A Chronicle of Volcanadas

A Chronicle of Volcanadas

Created and written by the warped mind of Josiah Shultz.

Illustrations by Isaac Shultz and Kieren Shultz

Creative consultations by Solomon Shultz

Co-edited by Mariah Shultz, Lily Shultz, and Isaac Shultz

(It's a lot simpler if you keep it all in the family)

(Oh look! More Shultz's)

Dedicated to Brett and Gina Shultz.

Y'know, because they raised me.

Contents

Author's Note

It is likely that many aspects of this story will seem familiar to you. Greed-driven villains. Unlikely heroes. Adventurous quests. These elements are common to many stories and mine is no exception. My goal in writing this story was primarily to prove that I was capable of doing so. But along the way, I realized that there was something greater I could achieve with my writing.

Having worked in a community library, I have observed firsthand the types of books circulating among American youth. So many of the stories being printed for young people today share a trend of darkness. Negative themes, explicit illustrations, and coarse language seem to be the order of the day.

My intention with this story is to communicate values that I believe are worth aspiring to. Behaviors such as loyalty, chivalry, and honor are what should be emphasized. Hopefully this story does justice to the value of these morals.

This is my first book, so don't judge it too harshly. If you like the story, tell the world. If you don't like it, keep your opinions to yourself.

A Chronicle of Volcanadas

Chapter 1

The Beginning

I am Jairus, the eldest son of Jabirus who was the son of Jairo. My father and his father before him were great generals. Leaders of men tasked with commanding the legions of Volcanadas. My father in particular proved himself to be exceptional as a warrior and tactician. His gift for strategy coupled with his forceful nature earned him the position of legion master at the young age of only one-score and two, an unusual feat for that time. It was because he was so highly distinguished that he was allowed the acquaintanceship of lady Magdalyn, the second daughter of Lord Enos, High King of the Volcanadian people. Acquaintanceship soon led to… other things… and it was the union of Jabirus and Magdalyn that begat my brothers, sisters, and myself. I am the eldest among the male offspring as I have already stated but am not the firstborn as I arrived second to my older sister. After me there came two brothers and four sisters for a sum total of seven children born to Jabirus and Magdalyn of Volcanadas.

You have probably made the assumption that I am a prince, and right that you should, since I have disclosed that I am the son of a princess. The title is mine and I shall carry it my whole life, however it does little more than signify that I am a member of the fairly large royal family. Lord Enos is High King and his only son Eber is the crown prince in line for the throne. Even if some ill happening were to befall Eber, I have three cousins who are in line for the crown ahead of me. I don't mean for this to sound like my eye is on the King's chair. To be perfectly honest I have no craving for the responsibilities of the position. I am perfectly content to follow in my father's footsteps and be trained in the defense of this magnificent kingdom. Speaking of which, I should quit boring you with all this talk about myself and share with you some of the proud history of Volcanadas.

One can never tell what you might find drifting on the surface of the ocean. The flotsam and jetsam swirling about, tossed and turned and tossed again by the ceaseless drifting of the waves. That is what my ancestors were, the debris of a dozen realms set adrift on an endless sea. A conglomeration of castoffs in a fleet of mismatched ships and vessels. They banded together for safety and support with little in common besides the fact that none of them knew where they were going. Every member of the party was lost in some way. Some had been at sea so long that they didn't know where they were from. For those with the ability to remember, there was the pain of knowing they could never return to their place of origin. When the seafarers landed on the shores that would become their new home, the majority failed to see the merits of staying and wished to move on. One man had the wisdom to recognize the unique benefits of this region's topography, and the foresight to realize the potential for this new place. This man was called Enochulus.

Enochulus was a philosopher, scientist, and religious leader among the people. It was at his request that the convoy had stopped along the coast of this new world. Furthermore, after a day of reconnoitering, he strenuously insisted that this was the safe haven our people had been searching for. Some called Enochulus daft for suggesting such a thing. As one might presume from the name, Volcanadas is built on and around an immense volcano. Who would be crazy enough to make their home on the side of a mountain that spurts fire and brimstone? This very question was put forth to Enochulus and his response was simple: "I would" he said.

Enochulus was unable to convince many of the travelers and they restocked their vessels and moved on. Those that stayed would be rewarded, for Volcanadas (as the region would be called) was more bountiful than even Enochulus had anticipated. The first attribute of the volcano that was so appealing was the lay of the land surrounding it. The area is highly defensible as it has formed into a natural fortress. The land itself is absolutely perfect for growing things due to the abundant nutrients in the volcanic soil. And though many had reservations about the volcano itself and the inferno it contained, the fire within the mountain would become the lifeblood of our people. While the main party went to work constructing a settlement, Enochulus took a smaller party and began doing experiments with the volcano. He worked zealously night and day and the fruits of his labor would benefit all. He believed that by facilitating the relief of the volcano's internal pressures we could prevent undesirable eruptions and channel the energy from the release. A result of Enochulus's experiments was an unlimited supply of steam power. Over time, Enochulus would create various machines to aid in the construction of our city. The first was a steam-powered towrope to be used in hauling building materials up the mountain. Next came a steam-saw for the newly constructed sawmill. Eventually, individual homes were fitted to have steam channeled in for warmth and hot water.

Another gift of the volcano discovered by Enochulus was the existence of diamonds. Mining operations were organized and underway by the second year in Volcanadas. Our people were thriving, and a new culture was in the making. As the settlement grew, it became clear that a leader was needed to guide the future of Volcanadas. Enochulus was the obvious choice and no one opposed his nomination. He graciously accepted and was crowned the first King of the Volcanadians.

Chapter 2

A Great Day to be Alive

The first signs of morning are just beginning to show along the horizon. The new day holds much to do, and I like to get an early start.

Jairus dressed in his usual attire, a loose-fitting long sleeve shirt, pantaloons held up by a thick leather belt, and sharkskin boots. He secured his favorite knife into a scabbard in his right boot and moved over to his balcony. His room was positioned on the eastern side of his parent's manor house and rested on the third floor. Without a moment's hesitation, he grabbed a thick rubber cord that was secured to the balcony railing and vaulted over into open space. The feeling of falling was something Jairus had always loved. The sensation made him feel alive and he did this nearly every morning. His rapid descent was slowed by the rubber cord and he landed neatly in his mother's garden. The second his feet touched the ground, he released the cord, allowing the elasticity to jerk it back up to the balcony where it would be ready for use in the future. Jairus sprinted through the garden grabbing a piece of fruit from one of the trees as he went. He left the garden and continued on down a path that would lead him out of the city. As he jogged, he looked further up the mountain to admire King Enos's castle. The magnificent palace had no equal as far as he knew.

His jaunt continued out of the city and around the side of the mountain where he stopped at the top of a sheer cliff. He took a deep breath, filling his lungs with the fresh sea air. Next, he kicked off his boots and removed his shirt and pants leaving him wearing only a pair of undershorts. He used his belt to cinch his clothes into a bundle which he then dropped over the side of the cliff to a small beach far below. With that done, he moved over to a small cave entrance partially concealed by boulders and went inside. The cave narrowed to a tunnel which then widened into a fairly large cavern. In the center of the cavern floor was a large hole about twelve feet across: a lava tube. Jairus smiled in anticipation as he picked up a long board with metal wheels fastened to the underside, one of several leaning against the wall. He stepped to the edge of the hole, and after pausing to take another deep breath, he held the board in front of him and dropped headfirst into the tube.

The freefall was short-lived. After a second or two he heard the sound of the metal wheels against stone. Jairus sped through the tube carved in a time long past by a burning stream of molten lava. He continued to pick up speed as daylight became visible at the end of the tunnel. In spite of the fact that he had done this several times before, the elation he felt was almost unbearable. He whooped and hollered at the top of his lungs to release some of the exhilaration he felt. As he shot out of the tube's exit, he glided through the air carried forward by his momentum; and for a moment, time seemed to stand still. He shoved his board away from himself and looked down at the waves beneath him. The water shimmered like gold in the early morning light. *Yes, it truly is a great day to be alive.* He stretched his arms above his head and dropped into a dive that broke cleanly through the surface of the sea. A moment later he emerged from the cool clear water and took in great gulps of air. Then he swam to his floating board and pushed it ahead of him as he kicked his way to the seashore. Upon reaching the beach, he stashed the board behind an outcropping of rocks along with the two boards from yesterday and the day before. Then, still concealed behind the outcropping for the sake of modesty, he changed his sea-soaked shorts for the pair he had left to dry the previous morning. With that done, he walked up the beach to retrieve the rest of his clothes.

Even among my fellow Volcanadians this is somewhat of an odd way to start the day. But what can I say? I like a little excitement. And if you start your morning with a little enthusiasm it gives the whole day a brighter appearance. Now I need to hurry and get back up to the city. I have my daily training with Leif and Bartimaeus and they won't let me hear the end of it if I'm late again. It's a fairly long hike and it will give me plenty of time to share some more with you about the reign of Enochulus.

In the years that followed the coronation of Enochulus there was much prosperity in our land. Travelers on land and sea stumbled across the newly formed kingdom and added to the population. Farming in the surrounding countryside flourished and fishing operations brought in a steady supply of the ocean's bounty. The mines supplied diamonds by the barrel and artisans crafted them into magnificent works of art and ornamentation. Things were good, but all v not absolutely perfect. For example, the mixture of the cool sea air with heat from the volcano produces a thick fog that surrounds the mountain much of the time. The moisture wreaks havoc on anythi metal in the form of corrosion and any untreated wood will almost surely become rotten to the core. Another problem is the flareflies, a bug averaging two-and-half to

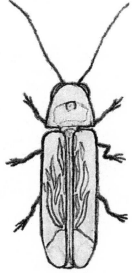

A Flarefly

three inches long and the thickness of a man's thumb. They feed exclusively on smaller insects which is a good thing in of itself. However, the flarefly has two characteristics that make it somewhat of a bother. First is the nasty little creature's bite. They are typically very peaceful and will not attack unless provoked, but when they do attack the effects are unmistakable. The flarefly possesses a venom containing a paralytic agent that brings almost immediate results. One bite can lay a full-grown man flat for five hours. The effect of such a bite on a small child would almost certainly be fatal. Miraculously enough, this tragedy has never taken place in our recorded history. It is as if the creatures comprehend what their venom is capable of and choose not to use it at times. The second characteristic is a bit more bothersome than the first and is also the inspiration for the name "flarefly." Contained within the thorax of the insect is a remarkable chemical substance that is subject to instantaneous combustion when oxygen is introduced. Piercing or rupturing a flarefly's thorax produces a small but intense flashfire. The problem associated with this is that it tends to a cause a multitude of accidental fires. Rain barrels and buckets are placed in strategic locations all around the kingdom for the purpose of fire suppression.

Even with the few detractions, Volcanadas continued to grow with increasing speed, but all this growth and prosperity couldn't help but attract negative attention. For years there were frequent raids from seafaring brigands. They would land on our beaches and try to ascend the volcano to pillage the settlement. A stop was put to this by the genius of King Enochulus. Several openings were made in the seaward side of the volcano. The next time the raiders landed on the beach, Enochulus triggered a small eruption that was directed through the newly created vents. A cloud of ash, rock, and magma spewed out over the beach. The Brigands that weren't killed by the blast retreated to their ships only to find that several of them had caught fire because of the flaming debris. Forced to abandon their blazing vessels, the marauders crowded themselves onto the remaining ships and fled. There were few attempts to attack from the sea after that.

The next problem to contend with was attacks on land. When the raiders approached the settlement from the south there were fewer obstacles. An eruption couldn't be used for defense on this side of the volcano because it would destroy the settlement. Enochulus had foreseen this and had organized the construction of a defensive wall along the volcano's southern side. This wall was defensible long before the land attacks had begun, but the problem was being able to defend it. The Volcanadian defenders were neither equipped nor trained well enough to fight the brigands head to head. Enochulus found a way to remedy this enigma in form of another steam-powered contraption. He devised a machine with a metal container in which to build up steam pressure. Attached to the compressor was a length of hose through which a fog of super-heated steam could be sprayed scalding anyone unfortunate enough to be in its path. With several of these fantastic machines at the disposal of the guardians, defending the wall from attackers became somewhat easier. The defenses of Volcanadas would only grow more impregnable.

Chapter 3

After Enochulus

Jairus jogged to the entrance of the courtyard of Enos's castle where Bartimaeus and Leif were waiting. Before he entered he could hear the distinctiv clashing of steel against steel hintii that his friends had begun without him. Jairus passed through the entry and saw that this was indeed the case. His comrades were facin off with each other in the cordonec off sparring area exchanging

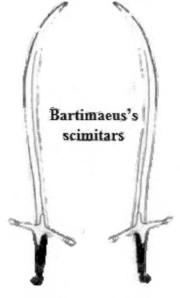

Bartimaeus's scimitars

elaborate combinations of cuts, slashes, and thrusts. Bartimaeus was using a matched pair of scimitars and Leif countered with his own heavy two-edged longsword. Jairus went and retrieved his own weapons from a storage room just off the courtyard. His primary weapon of choice was a long, straight-bladed rapier. In addition, he typically carried a pair of heavy-bladed short swords as secondary weapons.

Leif's Broadsword

When he returned to the courtyard, he leaned against the castle wall and watched as the sparring continued between the two boys. "The winner gets to spar with me" Jairus called to them with a smile.

"Oh! So you finally decided to show up" Leif responded in jest, his eyes still locked on his opponent. "Well I think we know who the winner will be" he boasted, just before he laid into Bartimaeus with a brutal combination.

The attack wrenched the sword from the smaller boy's left hand, sending it clattering across the cobblestones. Bartimaeus huffed in exasperation as ᴴe clutched his remaining sword with both hands.

**Jairus's
Rapier**

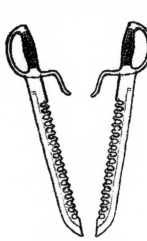

**Jairus's
Short-swords**

ᴜrty is a fair swordsman, but he is ʳly outmatched by Leif. The latter ʰas a distinct advantage in size, ᴺg over six feet and weighing two- ᴵ and fifty pounds. Broad in the ᴥ s and not lacking in muscle, Leif is surely a force to be reckoned with. Bartimaeus in comparison stands about a head shorter than Leif and could be described as having a wiry build. I am somewhat in between the two, standing just under six feet and possessing a lean frame. The three of us share the same year of birth, albeit several months apart, meaning that before the year is out we will all have reached sixteen years of age.

The match between the two friends continued for several more minutes. Leif delivered an onslaught of powerful blows met by Bartimaeus who countered with precision and finesse. I silently hoped that Barty might come out the victor as he has endured countless sessions with Leif and not once been the winner, but at least for today it was not to be. Leif swung a heavy cut towards Bartimaeus' sword and, at the last instant, incorporated a peculiar twist of his blade. This lightning fast maneuver effectively caught Barty off guard and sent his scimitar flying through the air.

We spent the next hour sparring like we've done every morning since we were eight. Then the following two hours were spent training and drilling with a group of younger boys who had been assigned to us. Ever since the reign of Enochulus, our culture has put great emphasis on military training. The defense of our city, the security of the kingdom, and the very survival of our people depends on our ability to protect ourselves. Every male child begins swordsman training at eight years of age. Volcanadas does not require that every boy join the military, but the idea is that every boy will be a capable fighter by the time they reach manhood. Ladies are encouraged to join the training as well since proficiency with a sword is not just valuable among men. After swordsman training was finished for the morning, we all walked as a group to the firing range on the northern edge of the city. Traditionally the range was used for archery practice but in recent years it has been used for a different training.

Lord Enos has a brother named Eros. The both of them are the great-great-grandsons of King Enochulus, the founder of Volcanadas. Eros, following in the footsteps of Enochulus, is the kingdom's volcano master and resident inventor. Eros was always fascinated by the flareflies that inhabit our mountain. He believed that there were many potential applications for the insect that had not as of yet been realized. Eros began experimenting with designs for a weapon that utilized the unique attributes of the flarefly, the result of these experiments would be revolutionary. The weapon would be called the flare-launcher, an invention composed of a smooth-bored steel tube fixed on a frame of wood or bone. It's a breech-loading weapon charged by opening the chamber at the base of the tube and inserting a parchment-wrapped cartridge. This cartridge consists of an average sized flarefly (with the legs and antenna removed) and a mixture of powdered magnesium and other flammable elements. The triggering mechanism of the flare-

launcher is a small lever that protrudes from the underside of the breech. Pulling the trigger backward forces a long needle into the chamber where it pierces the cartridge and the flarefly inside. The resulting explosion within the chamber launches the remaining portions of the insect through the barrel where it exits the other end as a deadly projectile. The original flare-launcher was easy to load, accurate to about thirty paces, and could be reloaded for another shot in five seconds.

A weapon such as this was unknown in our world and stimulated great excitement. Volcanadas now had an advantage in warfare that would be the envy of all the surrounding nations. Shortly after Eros unveiled his creation, a small modification was suggested by our champion Yeoman. Just as the fletching of an arrow makes it fly straighter, putting a spin on the projectile fired from the flare-launcher would increase both velocity and accuracy. At this suggestion, flare-launchers were manufactured with a rotating groove, or rifling in the barrel to improve accuracy. This led to a special adjustment in the preparation of the flare cartridge. The head of the flarefly would now be coated with a layer of soft metal that would take better to the rifling. The application of this coating also enabled cartridge makers to more precisely match the size of the flarefly with the diameter of the flare-launcher barrel. Rifled flare-launchers with the new style of cartridge now had a range of one-hundred-fifty paces making it even more formidable as a weapon. You may think it is cruel to use the creatures in this way. Ripping their legs off, dipping their heads in molten lead, and all so we can use them as a projectile. Put your mind at ease, for we do not kill the flareflies to use them as ammunition.

The flarefly has a comparatively short lifespan of just a few weeks and the bodies of those that die are left lying about all around the volcano. Every day, children are sent out to gather the dead insects and deliver them to the armory where the cartridges are made and stored. The creatures are treated with the utmost respect, in fact they are honored in culture. Every citizen of Volcanadas is expected to be capable of loading and firing a flare-launcher. The reason for this is again for the security of our city. The walls of Volcanadas have not been breached since the introduction of Enochulus's steam sprayer. But if ever this calamity occurs, a flare-launcher will be aimed and ready in the doorway of every household.

Chapter 4

A Routine Existence

*The three of us and our pupils spent the next hour
drilling on the loading, firing, and cleaning of the weapons.
After we had finished and put away the launchers, Leif and
Barty came with me to my parent's house for the midday meal.
Our cook had made one of my favorite things. A seasoned patty
of ground meat cooked over a fire and served on a fresh roll
with cheese, lettuce, and onion. After we finished eating, we
reported to the captain of the guard to get assigned our
positions for a three-hour shift on the city wall. I don't mind
being on sentry duty. I spend the time staring into the distance
imagining what lies beyond the boundaries of the kingdom. Like
the far-off lands across the prairies to the west or the
unexplored regions to the south. I was daydreaming about
things such as this when a melodious voice broke my train of
thought.*

"Good day Jairus" the voice said.

*I knew exactly who the voice belonged to even before I turned
around. It was Joanna, daughter of General Johannes, a good
friend of my father's.*

*The first time I saw her was in the castle courtyard. I
was seven years old and playing with Leif and Bartimaeus.
Joanna was six and asked if she could play too. We told her that*

we were heroes, she was a prisoner, and one of us was going to save her. We also told her that to be a good prisoner she would have to let us tie her up. She was willing, and so we used our belts to tie her to a hitching post. You might say that after that we forgot about her. It might also be true that she was tied to the post for over an hour. When it was time to go home, I realized I didn't have my belt and went looking for it. When I went back to the courtyard there she was, waiting patiently, and she gave me a big smile when she saw me coming. When it occurred to me just how cruel we had been to her, I felt so guilty that I almost turned and left again, but I forced myself to face her. "You kinda forgot me, didn't ya?" she asked after I untied the belts. "I did" I admitted, hanging my head with

shame. "But I swear I'll never forget you again." She thought this over for a moment, and then simply said "good" after which she turned and went home. From that day forward, I always made sure to include her whenever she wanted.

Joanna's Sabre

It has been about nine years and Joanna and I have both matured considerably. Now fifteen years old, Joanna has grown to be quite beautiful (though I have yet to tell her so). She stands about five and a half feet with her boots on and possesses a slim, yet full figure. Her eyes are the color of the sea on a stormy day and her hair is a golden brown like wheat that's ready for harvest. Spending so much time romping with me and my friends made Joanna more rough-and-tumble than lady-like. That is not to say that she behaves improperly for a girl, it's just that few girls keep up so well with the boys. Joanna is never seen without her sabre at her side and she is quite accomplished as a knife thrower. Furthermore, there is not a finer shot with a flare-launcher in all the kingdom.

"Good day milady" I said with a slight bow. "What brings you to the wall on this fine day?"

"Oh, I don't know. Just thought I would swing by and catch you napping" she quipped with a smile.

Jairus returned the smile but said nothing. He had found that it was growing increasingly difficult to speak with Joanna when the two of them were alone. He truly enjoyed her company, he just couldn't think of anything to say to her. For several minutes there was silence as Jairus stood his post while Joanna paced to and fro along the battlements.

"Where do you go every morning?" She asked, breaking the silence.

"Huh? What?'' Jairus responded.

Joanna sprung lightly up onto the nearest opening of the battlements and turned to look down at the confused Jairus.

"Every morning you jump from your balcony and go dashing off" she explained. "Where do you go?"

Jairus' face reddened slightly at the thought that she had been observing him. "I like to start my morning with a swim," he stated timidly.

"Oh" she said with interest. "Do you go anywhere special?"

"I have a particular spot" he offered vaguely.

She smiled at his hesitance. "I like to swim" she said.

Jairus said nothing, but he knew where she was headed.

"Maybe… I could go with you sometime?" she pressed.

Jairus found that he was having just a little trouble breathing, but he managed to gasp out a reply. "Perhaps" he said.

Joanna smiled with satisfaction and hopped down from the battlement.

"Good day" she said as she sauntered off along the wall.

I finished my shift on the wall with no excitement other than the visit from Joanna. There are few things that truly frighten me and being alone with her is one of them.

I went from the wall to King's stables where I saddled a mount to go for a ride. We don't have many horses in Volcanadas and the few that we have are imported

A Unihorn

from distant lands. A different type of creature acts as our primary beast of burden. It is a bit larger than a horse, and it doesn't have hooves. A visiting dignitary compared it to a creature called a rhinoceros, which he described as a massive animal with a tough gray hide and a horn on its snout. The

creatures here have more variance in color, the legs are longer in proportion to their bodies, and they are also a bit less bulky. They do have the same basic head shape complete with a horn.

The plains to the west are home to thousands of these brutes. They roam in vast herds and graze the grasslands and prairies. During the reign of Enochulus, farmers captured a number the animals and domesticated them. Some they raised for slaughter to provide red meat for the kingdom, others they trained to pull wagons and carts, and still others were broken to saddle. The unihorn (as we chose to call them) that I saddled for today's ride is a big black-coated beast with a horn over a foot in length. I mounted and rode to the city's southwestern gate and spurred to a gallop as we passed through. I steered my mount for the open prairies and was soon plowing through tall grass that brushed against my feet in the stirrups. The sun overhead shone brightly in a cloudless blue sky. I take a ride much the same as this nearly every day. After an hour or so, I returned to the stables and rewarded the faithful beast with thorough rubdown and a stick of caramelized honey.

That evening, Leif and Bartimaeus accompanied me once again at my home for dinner. Also joining us was Leif's family. Leif's father Liras had been killed in a cave-in at the diamond mines several years ago. Ever since the tragedy had occurred, Leif, his mother, and eleven siblings had been given a standing invitation to meals at the house of Jabirus and Magdalyn. Bartimaeus shares this invitation as well since both of his parents were killed in an accident; a fire caused by an electrical storm. Bartimaeus was just an infant at the time of the catastrophe and he was claimed by none other than Eros, the brother of King Enos. Eros was a widower with no child of his own and stepped eagerly into the task of raising the boy. Bartimaeus and the inventor have become the best of friends and I don't doubt that Barty will follow in Eros's footsteps as the next volcano master. The whole lot of us sat down to a feast of unihorn steaks, mashed potatoes with gravy, mixed vegetables, and fresh rolls. Everyone ate their fill as we enjoyed discussion of the day's events. Afterwards, all of us gathered in our reading room where father led us in our daily study of the scriptures.

When the evening's affairs had ended I took a shower in our indoor bathing room before retiring to my quarters. I laid out the clothes I would wear in the morning, replaced my knife on the stand next to my bed, and checked that the rubber cord on the balcony was still secure. In case you haven't noticed, I am quite the creature of habit. One day is essentially the same as the next. My daily routine is fairly fast-paced but it is routine nonetheless. I crave excitement, adventure, a rush if you will. The entire kingdom of Volcanadas exists in much the same way that I do, where everything is a routine. I thank God for all we have, for the seemingly boundless prosperity that Volcanadas is blessed with. But what bothers me is this: all good things come to an end and dark days are bound to come. Will we be ready when they do? Will I be ready?

Chapter 5

Dark Days

I woke before dawn and dressed for another day in clothes much the same as the day before. I sheathed my knife in my boot as I stepped to the balcony and grabbed the length of rubber. I dropped into the darkness of the garden below and was startled out of my wits to see Joanna waiting for me not two steps from where I landed. I was so caught off guard that I neglected to release my grip on the rubber cord. Having been stretched to its limit, the cord snapped back with full force, jerking my feet back up off the ground. Realizing my mistake an instant too late, I let go only to come crashing down flat on my back at Joanna's feet.

"Oh! You're early today" she observed. "Sorry if I scared you… I brought breakfast!" she added cheerfully.

"So I see" Jairus said as he got to his feet. "So… I guess you're… coming along for a swim?" he asked.

"Well… only if you don't mind" she said timidly.

"No… uh? That's fine. You can come along" he stammered.

"Great!" she responded happily. She handed him a small bundle and turned to jog off through the garden. Jairus followed after her, opening the bundle as he went. It contained half a dozen sweet rolls, still hot from the oven and glistening with melted butter. "This is going to be an interesting day" he thought.

Joanna maintained the lead until they got to the edge of the city. From there she followed Jairus along his usual path around the mountain. They didn't speak much, they just moved along steadily sharing the sweet rolls as they went. When they reached the edge of the cliff that overlooked Jairus' cove, he gestured with a sweep of his arm.

"This is it" he said.

Joanna looked at him incredulously, stepped to the edge to look down, and then looked back at him with wide eyes. "You dive off of this?" She asked in disbelief.

"Not quite" Jairus answered with a smile. He stripped to his shorts (with a bit of hesitance) and dropped his clothes over the side before he motioned for her to follow him. He then led her to the cave entrance and guided her through the tunnel to the lava tube. She gazed down into the deep, dark hole.

"This really doesn't look any better" she said.

"You could just watch from up here and then head back to the city" Jairus suggested.

Joanna mulled this over for a moment and then stepped outside the cave. She returned a moment later wearing just her shirt and undershorts. "I'll do it if we can go together" she stated.

It was probably a bad idea. I had never tried it with more than one person. But the next thing I knew, I was standing on the edge of the tube with the board in front of me and Joanna clinging to my back. On the bright side, if this failed terribly and we both died, I wouldn't have to worry about how extremely uncomfortable I felt with this young lady wrapped around my neck. Joanna doesn't weigh very much, but when our wheels hit stone and her body crushed down on me, I thought I felt a couple of ribs crack. To make things worse, the faster we went the louder she screamed. I couldn't breath and it was likely that I'd be deaf by the time we exited the tube. Yet despite the pain and suffering, I realized that there was nowhere else I would rather be. I was doing something I love with a person I really enjoy being with. What could possibly be better than that? We shot from the tube like a flarefly from a launcher. I pushed off from the board and Joanna pushed off from me. We hit the water synchronously and resurfaced a moment later. Joanna laughed with delight. "We have to do that again!" she shouted. I nodded in agreement, ignoring the ache in my chest and the ringing in my ears. This was a magical moment, with the two of us together and her so pretty. She truly was beautiful with her wet hair shimmering in the light of the approaching dawn. Unfortunately, the moment was cut short as a deafening boom shattered the beauty of the morning.

Chapter 6

Honor Bound

They raced to the shore as fast as they could and scrambled to retrieve their clothes. The boom had come from the volcano which was now billowing with a cloud of steam and ash. This was not an eruption or a scheduled pressure release, this was a sign of distress. This plume was to signify some tragedy or alert the people to a state of emergency. When both were fully dressed, they turned and ran as fast as they could to get back to the city. When they reached the nearest gate, they stopped to catch their breath and Jairus called up to the guard on the wall.

"What's happened? What's wrong?" He hollered.

"I don't know, I haven't heard yet" the sentry replied.

Jairus and Joanna set out once again, cutting between houses and running through the streets. As they came around the side of a building, a unihorn bolted past with Bartimaeus atop the saddle.

"Bartimaeus!" Jairus hollered. Barty hauled back on the reigns to bring his mount to a stop and turned to acknowledge whoever had hailed him.

"What's happened?" Joanna called out.

"Lord Enos received a dispatch from King Rotiart of Layatreb. They are being attacked by the Alfabetians under King Eleminos and request our assistance. You need to speak to your father, and you to yours" he said to Jairus and then Joanna. With that, Bartimaeus returned his attention to whatever errand he was on and galloped off.

During the reign of Edwalpa, the son of Enochulus, a new enemy emerged from the kingdom of Alfabetia in the northwest. The Alfabetians were an extremely militant people from a growing empire. The leaders of this war-hungry nation set their sights on the wealth that could be gained in the acquisition of Volcanadas. Another kingdom that was growing to the north was the small but prosperous realm of Layatreb. It was Edwalpa's idea that an alliance be formed between Volcanadas and Layatreb. And so it was that in times of trouble against a common enemy such as the Alfabetians the Volcanadians and Layatrebians would come to the aid of each other. This worked out quite well for both nations and it was seldom that any actual aid had to be given; now appeared to be one of those rare occasions that it was necessary.

When Joanna and Jairus reached the castle, they split up to search for their respective fathers. Jairus was scanning a crowded meeting hall within the castle when a hand grabbed his shoulder and he turned to see that his father had found him.

Jabirus' face was clouded with concern as he led his son to an alcove where they could talk privately.

"According to Rotiart's dispatch, the entire Alfabetian army is bearing down on Layatreb." Jabirus said. "Enos has ordered all the legions of Volcanadas to be ready to march this afternoon. Enos himself will be leading us and Eber will be at his side."

"Father" Jairus interrupted. "Please say that I am coming with you."

Jabirus sighed deeply and placed his hands on his son's shoulders. "The defense of Volcanadas falls to the home-guard, of which you are a member. Your duty lies here my son, do not underestimate its importance."

The next afternoon found Jairus astride a unihorn patrolling the outlying regions of the kingdom with Leif and Bartimaeus. The legions of Volcanadas had departed on schedule in the early afternoon of the previous day. Jairus had watched them leave from the city wall along with all the other members of the home-guard. The guard consisted mostly of retired soldiers, female volunteers, and young trainees that had not yet achieved warrior status. Jairus fell into the latter category, along with Barty, Leif, and Joanna. Their duties include manning the watchtowers, keeping wall sentries posted round-the-clock, and riding the perimeter as they were doing now. Nobody expected any trouble to come knocking here because the real trouble was with the Alfabetians in Layatreb, but they made sure to keep on guard just in case.

We had been out for nearly two hours and had seen nothing but jackelots hunting rodents in the tall grass. We moved on to check the unihorn herds to the southwest of the city when one of the herders hailed for us to stop.

"Rustlers" he shouted when he got within earshot.

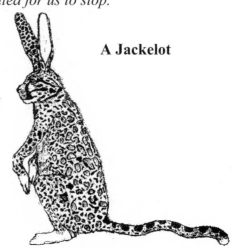

A Jackelot

Unfortunately, rustling had become increasingly common in recent years. Even though wild unihorns on the plains were free for the taking, Volcanadian unihorns were very highly sought after. Those that we domesticated and raised for meat tended to have less gristle than their wild counterparts. And breaking a wild unihorn to saddle was a long and dangerous process. "How many were there" I asked the man as he drew closer.

"Five or six" he replied. "We wanted to take off after them but we're shorthanded out here. The scum managed to cut two-dozen head from the rest of the herd before we knew what was happening."

"How long has it been and where did they run to?" Bartimaeus inquired.

"They were riding due west and it was less than half an hour ago" the herder answered.

"Check the loads in your launchers" I told the others.

In addition to our assorted bladed weapons, each of us had a full-size flare-launcher slung across our backs and two more short-barreled launchers in holsters on our saddles. After receiving a nod of affirmation from both of my companions, I kicked my unihorn to a gallop with Leif and Bartimaeus at my heels.

Chapter 7

Unforeseen Circumstances

"Jair, hold up" called Bartimaeus. Jairus reigned in his mount and turned in the saddle to face his friend. Bartimaeus looked troubled and unsure.

"Something isn't right. I don't know what it is, but something is not right" Bartimaeus said seriously.

Jairus looked at Leif who gave a knowing nod. They both knew that Bartimaeus had a gift for sensing trouble. Long ago they had realized the importance of paying heed to his intuition.

"We'll drop smoke for reinforcements and move ahead slowly until they get here" Jairus said.

His companions nodded their agreement and Leif pulled a parcel from his saddle-bag. Inside the package was a mineral compound that produces a thick green smoke when burned. Leif pulled a cord on the outside of the package that caused a flarefly to rupture on the inside. He dropped it to the ground as the package burst into flames and the three of them watched as the colored smoke climbed into the sky. Bartimaeus used a spyglass to look back toward the watchtower on the city wall. They stayed by the smoke until a matching plume began ascending from the watchtower in acknowledgment of their own signal. A contingent of ten mounted troops would come shortly to provide backup. Jairus took the lead as the three continued in pursuit of rustlers.

The trail of the stolen livestock led into the mouth of a little valley with high ridges on both sides. This type of terrain is ideal for an ambush thought Jairus, and he held up a clinched fist to call his friends to a halt. He signaled Leif to go up the rise to the right of the trail and Bartimaeus the left. He himself would enter the valley with his friends covering him from above. After giving the other boys a head start, Jairus urged his mount forward, anxious to see what was in store in the valley ahead. There was nothing amiss as far as Jairus could tell upon entering the basin, yet he began to feel an unwarranted tension building in his chest and he detected a similar uneasiness in the animal beneath him. Never one to shy from a challenge, Jairus held his flare-launcher at the ready and surged to the top of the next rise, thinking he was ready for whatever lay ahead. But he was wrong.

Jairus pulled back on the reigns, shocked and confused by what he saw at the base of the hill ahead of him. There was not a rustler in sight, but he had found the stolen unihorns. And he had found them dead. Nearly two-dozen of the beasts were strewn about, their thick hides riddled with arrows. Jairus gaped at the grisly slaughter of the poor brutes. So stunned was he by the picture before him that he failed to notice the rumble of hooves until the riders crested the ridge above him. No less than fifty riders, Alfabetian cavalry all armed to the teeth, and the whole horde bearing down on the lone Jairus.

"Lord protect us" he breathed. Spurring into action, Jairus dug his heels into his mount and wheeled the unihorn around to take flight. He grabbed his hunting horn off of his saddle and brought it to his lips to let off a long blast. If either of his friends had not yet spotted the enemy riders, this signal would tell them to retreat. He knew that they would likely have to stand and fight. Unihorns are built for endurance rather than speed, so the Alfabetian horses would have little trouble overtaking them. Even if they met up with the troop of reinforcements they would be grossly outnumbered. All these things ran through Jairus' mind as he emerged from the mouth of the valley onto the flatlands.

Leif and Bartimaeus were just ahead of him having spurred their mounts when they saw him approaching. Jairus stole a glance over his shoulder at the pursuing enemies. The Alfabetian archers were letting loose with a barrage of arrows in an effort to halt his attempt at escape. He actually saw the arrow that brought him down, a broad-head arrow that pierced his unihorn's left hind leg. The beast let out a shriek of pain and crashed to the ground sending Jairus flying headlong onto the grass. He scrambled to his feet and rushed back to where his fallen steed lay. Wincing at the pain the creature obviously felt, he moved to the saddle and withdrew the short launchers. He laid the two weapons within easy reach and knelt beside them. He brought his longer weapon to his shoulder and began firing, reloading, and firing again as fast as he could. He managed to shoot four of the attackers out of the saddle before the nearest rider reached his position. He dropped flat to the ground to avoid a downward slash of a sword and came up with a short launcher in each hand. He fired both simultaneously and two more riders fell. Looking up, he saw the cavalry troop was within seconds of running him into the dust. The nearest Alfabetian held an upraised javelin aimed at Jairus' heart and time slowed for an instant. As he breathed what he believed to be his final breath, his thoughts were with his father.

"Let him be safe" he prayed silently.

Just as the warrior was about to let the javelin fly, he was plowed over, horse and all by Leif atop his unihorn. Leif plunged into the throng of Alfabetians cleaving with the broadsword in his right hand and clubbing with the flare-launcher in his left. Bartimaeus appeared suddenly at Jairus' side, fired his two short-launchers and then drew his scimitars. Jairus drew his short swords as he jumped to his feet, then he and Bartimaeus ran side-by-side into the fray.

Three young Volcanadians pitted against fifty Alfabetians sounds like a pretty hopeless struggle, yet we seemed to be holding our end pretty well. Barty and I fought back to back, our years of training coming into play as we fought for our very lives. Leif was like an army of one. No enemy could get within five feet of him without receiving an injury or meeting death. More than twenty of the horse-soldiers lay dead or dying, but that still left the odds at nearly ten to one. Leif took an arrow through his left arm and I took a bad cut across my leg. All three of us were beginning to tire and it was looking as if the end was near. Then all of a sudden, a deafening boom split the air and eight of the remaining Alfabetians fell dead. Jairus' heart leapt with joy and he fought with renewed vigor. The reinforcement party had arrived at last with Joanna at the head of them. Another volley from the Volcanadians dropped seven more enemy troops. The Alfabetians turned to meet this counterattack which left the battered trio of friends with a moment to catch their breath. After a couple of minutes, all of the enemies had been vanquished and attention was refocused on tending wounds.

"You guys got yourselves in pretty deep trouble" Joanna commented to Jairus as she cinched a bandage over the wound on his leg. He winced slightly at the pain but smiled his appreciation of her care.

"We aren't the only ones who have had trouble!" Bartimaeus stated urgently. "Jairus! You take a look" he said as he handed over his spyglass.

Jairus took the glass and began scanning to the north. "We have two columns of red smoke to the north and north-east" he announced. "Red smoke means other attacks." His face was grave as he turned to look at all the others. "This is an invasion."

Chapter 8

A Breach of Defense

Ash and steam poured from our great mountain as a decree of emergency. We lit off a red smoke signal of our own and then mounted for the ride back to the wall. Bartimaeus and I jumped on the nearest Alfabetian horses since my unihorn was incapacitated and his had wandered off. Then I took the lead as we whipped our animals to a gallop. If this was a full-scale assault, then we had better reach the walls before the enemy cuts us off. "What does all this mean?" I wondered. "Were the Alfabetians just hanging around, waiting for our army to leave? Was the supposed attack on Layatreb just a ruse? A ploy to draw the Volcanadian complement away from the city?" These thoughts and questions were interrupted when I spotted a line of Alfabetian cavalry off on our left flank. I signaled my friends behind me to be sure they saw them as well. Then I realized that another enemy contingent was coming in from the right. They weren't attacking us. I don't think they had even noticed us yet. They were on course for the same gate of the city that we were aiming towards, and it was likely that their horses would get them there first. Looking ahead to the gate, I was horrified to see that it was standing wide open. Something must be wrong. The wall guards should have seen the oncoming attack. The gate would have to be closed or else a hundred Alfabetians would enter the city unchecked. I looked to Bartimaeus who had drawn even with me on my right and then I looked behind us at Leif, Joanna, and the others who were falling behind on the slower animals. Turning back to Bartimaeus, I yelled to him: "We have to close the gate." He nodded solemnly in response and we urged our horses to go as fast as possible. Knowing there was no way that they could make it, Joanna and Leif called their group to a halt as they watched Jairus and Bartimaeus race ahead.

At their quicker pace, it looked as though Bartimaeus and Jairus would reach the Gate just a few moments before the enemy soldiers. Some of the Alfabetians had realized this and started letting fly a few arrows from the backs of their galloping horses. The gate still stood open and there appeared to be a small battle raging on the wall. The mechanism that closed the gate seemed to be under enemy control.

"Let's see what I can do about that" Jairus muttered determinedly to himself. He drew his rapier as he charged through the gate and was nearly skewered to death by a civilian with a halberd. He managed to parry at the last possible second and avoided a blow that would have surely killed him. Bartimaeus came through the gate right after and threw himself from the saddle onto the man with the halberd. Jairus turned his mount back toward the wall-entrance and charged. Anticipating his friend's next action, Bartimaeus picked the fallen halberd up

from the ground and threw it into the air ahead of Jairus.
Dropping his rapier, Jairus grabbed the halberd and jumped
from his horse just as he reached the gate, slamming the halberd
into an opening between two stones in the wall. The long
weapon now stood out perpendicular to the wall with Jairus
hanging by its handle. He chinned himself up, hiked a leg onto
the haft, and thrust his body upward to grab a stone that jutted
out from the wall. Next, he reached up and dug his dagger into
the wall for another purchase. The knife from his boot served as
another. He was almost to the landing above the gate and the
Alfabetian cavalry had almost reached the wall. The gate
couldn't be closed in time, but he could still drop the portcullis.
Summoning all of his strength, he lunged up the last few feet of
wall and grasped the edge by his fingertips. A figure appeared
above him, another civilian, and he drew back with a sword to
hack Jairus from the wall. This action was cut short as
Bartimaeus' flare-launcher bucked, and the would-be assassin
fell dead. The muscles in Jairus' arms screamed as he dragged
himself up over the wall. He saw to his dismay that two more
foes stood between him and his goal, and the first half-dozen
Alfabetian cavalrymen were passing through the gate beneath
him. Jairus drew his short swords from the crisscrossed
scabbards on his back. As his two opponents charged, the young
Volcanadian let fly with the sword from his right hand. It sailed
past his startled foes and struck true against the lever that

released the portcullis. The wrought-iron gate fell, sweeping two enemy riders out of their saddles and crushing them beneath its weight. The entrance was secure.

I threw my body backward down the wall I had just scaled and caught hold of the halberd, then I dropped the rest of the way and rolled when I hit the ground. I jumped to my feet and turned to reassess the situation. Bartimaeus was still in the middle of the path with his knee in the back of the man who had tried to kill me at the gate. The few enemies that still held positions on the wall were being routed. Additional reinforcements were pouring in from all directions to repel the enemies at the gate. I ran to Bartimaeus, my thoughts with the comrades we had left outside the wall.

"We need to get the others inside" I shouted to Bartimaeus above the din of the battle.

"I know" Bartimaeus acknowledged, "but I have to get this man to Eros" he said as he dragged his prisoner to his feet.

I was about to ask what was so important about this prisoner when I spotted Drackus, the captain of the home-guard. I patted Bartimaeus' shoulder and rushed to speak with the old soldier.

"Report" *Drackus ordered when I approached him.*

"My patrol was engaged by enemy cavalry just before the attack began" I stated. "I came ahead to secure the gate and eleven members of my troop are trapped outside the wall."

The old soldier's face was grim. "There isn't anything we can do for them right now. I need you to go to the main gate and make sure our defenses are holding."

With that said, Drackus turned to deal with the next issue at hand and left me to do as I was told. I had no choice but to follow orders, so I went and retrieved my rapier from where I had dropped it earlier and headed off to the main gate.

Chapter 9

Treachery

Before long, the Alfabetians fell back to lick their wounds bringing the attack to an end for the day. We of the home-guard had plenty of wounds to tend to ourselves. In addition, ammunition supplies needed to be replenished and blades needed sharpened or replaced. I couldn't shake the feeling of guilt at leaving my comrades outside the wall. I had met with Drackus again to discuss the problem and we had come up with a plan. As soon as it was dark, I was going to slip over the wall and go looking for them. Now I just had to endure the maddening wait for nightfall. I decided to go looking for Bartimaeus and remembered how intent he had been on delivering that prisoner to Eros, so I set a course for the castle. When I got there, I asked where I could find Eros and was directed to his laboratory.

"Ah, Jairus! It is good that you are here." Eros exclaimed as I entered. "How goes the fighting?"

I gave them a brief summary of the current situation in terms of damages, wounded, and dead. "Now what is so important about this prisoner?" I asked, gesturing with my arm to the man bound hand and foot on the floor.

"Well aside from the fact that he nearly killed you," Bartimaeus began. "He happens to be the messenger who brought the dispatch from Layatreb. "

I was confused. "So, the dispatch was a forgery?" I queried.

"No" Eros replied. "The message was written in Rotiart's hand and sealed by his ring."

"What does this mean?" I asked Eros.

The prisoner spat in my general direction. "Stupid boy" he said. "You've been betrayed."

"Explain yourself" I ordered the captive, and he seemed only too glad to describe the plot. "High King Rotiart has struck a bargain with Lord Eleminos of the Alfabetians. According to the terms of the agreement, Alfabetia will open up a trade-route between Layatreb and the western territories in exchange for the deliverance of Volcanadas." *He grinned smugly as he said this, and I wanted so much to wring his scrawny neck.*

"Your King marches to his death" he continued. "When your legions reach Layatreb the gates will be locked to them and Eleminos will crush them. Then he will come here and finish what was started today."

"No!" I shouted, my face flushed with rage. "That isn't going to happen" I professed.

"Oh really" the man scoffed. "And the famed walls of Volcanadas will never be breached either. Well they were today!"

I dropped down to one knee to be at eye level with the man. "The only reason that happened is a snake like you held the door for them" I said, and I threw a punch at his nose for emphasis.

"Jairus! That's enough" Eros said. "He'll pay for what he's done in due time. We have more important things to attend to right now. Bartimaeus tells me that some of the guard didn't make it back inside the city before the attack."

"Yes sir" I replied. I'll be going out to look for them as soon as it gets dark."

"And I will be going with him" Bartimaeus added with conviction.

"No Bartimaeus" I said. "You'll likely be needed here, and..."

"And I" Bartimaeus interrupted, "would never forgive myself if I let you go alone."

I remained silent, as there was nothing I could think of to contest that.

"So, it's settled then" said Eros.

The night came, and we were ready. It was a full moon, but clouds filled the sky and blocked much of the light. A rope was dropped from between the battlements on the wall. Bartimaeus slid silently to the ground with me close behind him. We were dressed completely in black, right up to the hoods that covered our faces. After stopping for a moment to be sure that we had not been observed, we dashed out into the night. It would take much longer to get where we were going on foot, but the order of the day was stealth and silence. Just as our unihorns were left behind, so too were our flare-launchers. They make too much noise and draw far too much attention. Each of us carried a short bow as our primary weapon with a quiver of arrows slung over a shoulder. I had decided to leave my rapier at home as well but brought both of my short swords and an extra dagger; Bartimaeus had chosen to carry both of his scimitars. Enemy encampments dotted the plains outside the city with their campfires glowing in the night. We took our time as we weaved through the tall grass. Soon we had passed the farthest Alfabetian camp without incident. Now a new challenge lay ahead of us: finding our destination in the dark. I had been thinking about where our friends could be hiding and had remembered a cave that we had discovered years ago. Bartimaeus had been the one to actually find it, or more accurately, fall into it. We had been out exploring, him, Leif, and myself, and Barty had quite literally stumbled into it. It was a very deep cave, and the entrance could be easily missed. It was a perfect hiding spot, and Leif would certainly have thought of it when seeking refuge in the hills. The trouble is that we had not been to the cave in over a year and I was not completely sure that I could find it again, particularly at night. There was also a chance that the others had not found the cave either and were hiding someplace else. And then there was the possibility that I didn't want to consider: that they might have been captured or killed.

It has been four hours since we went over the wall. Bartimaeus and I have agreed that we are in the general vicinity of the cave. We had been debating whether or not it was safe to try calling out to our friends when we heard and felt the rumble of hooves. Taking cover in some brush, we watched as a group of Alfabetian horsemen topped the next rise and began heading in our direction. We dropped to the ground and waited as they passed, praying that we wouldn't be spotted by the light of their torches. When they had gone, the two of us got up and discussed what the horsemen were up too.

"I think that's a good sign" said Bartimaeus. "It looks as if we're not the only ones looking for Leif and the others, and that means they're still alive."

With that thought lifting our spirits, we headed off to continue our search. We hadn't gone far when I heard a distinctive grunt that most certainly came from a distant unihorn.

"There" I exclaimed. And began running in the direction the sound had come from. I slowed as we entered a small stand of trees and I stopped to listen. I was rewarded, not with the noise of an animal, but with the sight of steel glinting in the darkness as it sailed towards my head. I dropped to the ground as a dagger "thunked" into the tree just about where my head had been a moment before.

"Joanna!" I hissed loudly.

"Jairus?" She called back doubtfully.

"It's me" I said. "It wouldn't be me anymore if I hadn't seen your knife coming" I said indignantly.

I heard Bartimaeus snicker in the darkness behind me.

"Yeah, you can laugh" I said. "You're not the one whose head almost got lopped off."

Leif appeared at my side, looming in the darkness. "Quit complaining already and come inside."

Chapter 10

Forming a Plan

Ten minutes later we were galloping across the plains. Bartimaeus was riding double with Leif and I was situated behind Joanna. Leif had led the group directly to the cave, just as I had suspected, and they had remained hidden there all day. Now the plan was to ride due south until we were beyond the enemy patrols and then head east to the seashore. Waiting for us there, as per my arrangement with Drackus, was a boat that would come ashore to pick us up. After that it would just be a short ride back to the base of the volcano and the climb back up to the city. We went as far south as we thought necessary without running into any Alfabetian patrols and stopped to rest the unihorns for a while before heading east. We stopped for a rest under the cover of some trees. Joanna said she was going to backtrack on foot to double check that we weren't being followed and I volunteered to accompany her. We jogged to the top of the nearest rise and stopped at a cedar tree. Joanna shinnied up about halfway to afford a better view and dropped down a moment later having seen nothing.

"I want to apologize" I said as we began to walk back.

"What did you do?" she asked teasingly.

"I feel guilty for abandoning all of you outside the wall" I explained seriously. "I did what had to be done. I know that.

But if anything had happened to any of you I never would have forgiven myself."

Joanna stopped walking and just looked at me for a moment. "You're a good man Jairus" she said finally. "And someday, you'll make a great leader."

"I don't know about that" I countered.

"Maybe not" she said softly, "but I do."

A few short hours later we were back in Volcanadas. Leif and the others who had sustained wounds were sent to receive proper attention. The rest of us went to get some food before going to the guardhouse and collapsing for some well-earned rest. It seemed as if my eyes had only just closed when I was awakened by a hand on my shoulder. In reality, I had slept for four hours and it was nearly daylight. The fink who had awakened me up was Bartimaeus, who then told me that Eros had requested a conference with us. We were joined by Leif and Joanna, both of whom looked bleary-eyed and exhausted. Eros was looking rather ragged as well having slept little or not at all.

"Ah, children, thank you for coming" he said as we entered. *He motioned for us to sit down at a long table and laid a large map before us. He jammed a finger at the map between Volcanadas and Layatreb.*

"Enos is here" he said. "Our army will reach Layatreb in another three days and they will be facing the Layatrebian army as well as the main body of Alfabetia's forces." He looked up at each of us, probing for our thoughts with his eyes.

"So, what're we gonna do about it?" He asked.

No one said anything for a minute. Then I voiced my thoughts on the matter.

"It goes without saying that we need to alert Enos, so the real question is: how do we accomplish that? I think the fastest way would be for me to take a small boat and sail up the coast. I could beat the army to Layatreb and double back on land to intercept them."

Eros looked thoughtful as he considered my proposal.

"I disagree" Leif announced. "Going by sea would indeed be faster, but there is no guarantee that you'd get there. A small boat traveling up the coast is bound to get picked off by pirates. And even if you managed to get as far as Layatreb. You have no idea where enemy forces are encamped or what kind of patrols they have out."

"What do you propose instead Leif?" Eros inquired.

"I would go overland, either by stealing an Alfabetian horse or on a Unihorn. If all went well, I could overtake the army before they reach Layatreb."

"I don't see how that is any less dangerous" I said. "There are bound to be patrols along the roads. And there have been stories of highwayman attacking travelers."

"Both plans have their risks, and neither is perfect" Eros said. "No plan is ever foolproof, so I say we use both. Two of you will go by land and the other two by sea. Lord willing, both teams will reach Enos, but this way if one fails we can depend on the other. Are we agreed? Good, you leave within the hour."

Jairus jogged from the castle to his parent's house, his muscles still aching from the previous day. He passed through his mother's garden and entered the house via the kitchen entrance. He found his mother on the balcony of the master bedchamber, a spyglass held to her eye as she observed the distant enemies. She turned at his approach and he saw the fatigue from a sleepless night in her somber face. He melted into her warm embrace and held her tightly for a moment without speaking.

"I have a lot to tell you" he said softly. "And I don't have much time."

They settled in on his parent's bed and he told her of his part in previous day's events. As his report reached its end, he told her of the mission on which he was to embark. Though she tried to hide it, he could see the pain in her eyes at thought of the dangers involved in the mission. "Bring your father home" was all she said.

Bartimaeus had never been too keen on ocean travel so he would go with Leif on the overland route. I was to lead the sea team with Joanna as my partner. The sun was still low in the sky as the four of us set sail. Bartimaeus and Leif along with their unihorns and supplies would travel with us for about five miles

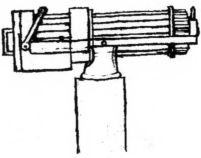

Eros's Swivel-Launcher

up the coast; then we would put them ashore and go our separate ways. Our boat was a small fifty-foot vessel with low draft and a single-mast. Our craft also had a special addition to the prow that would hopefully aid us against pirates. This contraption was a gift from Eros, a new invention of his. It consisted of ten flare-launcher barrels fixed to a rotating frame and mounted on a pedestal.

A canister with ten cartridge-chambers detached from the base of the barrels so that all ten chambers could be loaded at once. On the side of the pedestal was a lever that rotates and fires the barrels one after the other until all have been fired. All ten rounds could be fired in a matter of seconds. With extra canisters, this weapon was capable of firing nearly thirty rounds a minute. Leif and Barty were given a new toy as well. Eros had fashioned a metal can and pressurized it with some sort of flammable gas. Attached to the top of the can was a hose and at the end of the hose was a wick. The weapon is used by first lighting the wick and then opening a valve to release the gas. The result is a burst of flame that shoots six to eight feet from the end of the hose. One can of gas is only enough for about a minute of sustained flame, but it could still prove useful as a weapon or for creating a diversion. Leif and Bartimaeus each had two of these cans with the rest of their gear.

We reached the drop off point without incident and bid farewell and good luck to each other. The mission that lay ahead of us was unlike anything we had undertaken before. The four of us were young and inexperienced, but right now the future of our nation was dependent on us.

Chapter 11

Trials and Tribulations

Both Joanna and I are quite at home on the water. Seafaring is in our heritage and fishing is a significant part of Volcanadian culture. I love the roll of the deck beneath my feet and the salty spray carried by the wind against my face. Joanna has the agility of a cat when she's up on the mast and she works the sheets like an old salt. Together we make a fine team and fair seas lay ahead. We were making good time sailing up the coast periodically trading off at manning the tiller. We went through the morning and into the afternoon without seeing another vessel. We didn't talk much, and there really didn't seem to be much worth saying. The events that had transpired the previous day weighed heavily on our minds. And if Joanna is half as worried for her father as I am for mine, then it's a wonder that we haven't both succumbed to the stress. We ate a late lunch of some bread, cheese, and dried meat as we continued our trip. I was just beginning my third turn at the tiller when Joanna called down from her perch as the lookout.

"Craft approaching" she yelled. "It just came out of a cove up ahead and it looks like they mean business. *"*

"How many aboard?" I asked.

"It's about the same sized boat as ours. Probably seven or eight." She answered.

"Load up Eros's new launcher!" I called up to her. "I'm going to turn a few points to starboard to see if they shift their course, and if they do, open fire."

Joanna slid down a rope to the rolling deck and moved eagerly to the big multi-barreled launcher.

I turned our vessel angling it towards the open water and the boatload of brigands immediately changed course to intercept us.

"Big mistake" Joanna asserted. She rotated the crank on the big contraption and it fired three rounds in quick succession. "Cool!" she said giddily. And cranked out another seven rounds. She quickly detached the empty canister and replaced it with a full one. She opened fire once again and peppered the deck of the enemy boat. The pilot of the other craft seemed to take the hint that we wished to be left alone and turned back toward the beach.

"That was easy" said Joanna as she turned to face my position in the stern. *My blood ran cold as I looked past her to what lay ahead. "I don't think it's over yet" I said.*

After Leif and Bartimaeus had parted ways with Jairus and Joanna, the two of them had worked their way up from the beach to the flatlands above. They were just reaching the top of a rise and crested the hill atop their unihorns only to find themselves at the very edge of an enemy camp. Eight Alfabetians sat around a small cook-fire with their horses tied to a nearby picket line.

"Aww nuts" exclaimed Bartimaeus. As the enemy soldiers scrambled for their bows, Leif spurred his unihorn right through the center of the camp, trampling the men's breakfast as he went. He kept right on going and plowed through the picket line to scatter the horses. Bartimaeus fired his launcher over the heads of the archers to buy some time as he and Leif headed for hills.

"A ride with you is never boring" Bartimaeus called with a laugh.

Leif smiled back. "We should be well away by the time they catch their horses."

They continued west, ever watchful for enemy patrols and they traveled all morning without seeing another living soul. At midday they stopped at a stream to let the unihorns water and took the opportunity to have a quick lunch from their supplies. The break was kept short and they continued on into the afternoon. The plains gradually melted away into the thick forest known as the Dark Wood. The road to Layatreb cut through the eastern edge of the wood, but much of the interior was unexplored. It was reputed to be the home of thieves and highwaymen. Just before they entered the trees, Bartimaeus brought his unihorn to a sudden stop and called for Leif to do the same.

"What's wrong?" Leif asked.

"I don't know" Bartimaeus replied apprehensively. "I've just got that feeling again" he said. "Maybe we could head back towards the coast and avoid the forest."

Leif didn't like this idea at all. Circling around the forest would take hours of time that they couldn't afford to lose. "We'll just have to be careful" he said to Bartimaeus. "We don't have time to cut all the way around." He could tell that Barty was less than pleased with this response, but the decision was made and the two continued on.

Joanna turned with her spyglass to observe what I had spotted. "Warship, running full speed with her sweeps" she called with alarm.

"The first boat was just feeling us out. This one is coming to finish up" I said. "

With that many sweeps, there's at least thirty men aboard" Joanna predicted. "What are we gonna do?"

I thought hard before responding to her question. Turning around was no good because the wind would be against us. Running for open water would only get us so far, the rowers on the enemy vessel gave it too much speed.

"Open fire as soon as they get within range" I told her.

"I'm not sure how much good I can do" she replied. "The prow of the ship blocks my aim. I can't hit anything on the deck."

"Let'em have it anyway. Show them what that launcher is capable of. And try aiming for the sweeps. Maybe that will slow them down."

Joanna cranked for all she was worth, peppering the prow of the approaching vessel and chewing into the long wooden sweeps. Jairus tied off the tiller to keep them on course and opened the compartment that held their supplies. He quickly put together a haversack for each of them, putting in a short launcher with ammunition, some food, a water flask, and various other supplies. Then he rushed to the front of the boat to help reload the canisters Joanna had already used up.

As they enemy ship drew nearer, it was obvious that there was nothing more they could do.

"Help me tip this beast over the side" Jairus grunted, as he began to lift the big launcher from its pedestal. If their boat was going to be taken, at least Eros's invention wouldn't be captured along with it. The red-hot barrels of the contraption hissed with steam as it plunged beneath the waves. It made Joanna sad to see the brilliant weapon sink into the depths. Just before the warship pulled up next to their smaller vessel, Jairus and Joanna dove over the side. They stayed submerged as long as their lungs would allow and surfaced just long enough for a quick breath. They continued this practice as they made their way to the shore. In the meantime, the deck of their abandoned craft was swarmed by the pirates who were disappointed to find nothing of value. The brigands set the boat ablaze before retreating to their own craft, and a few moments later the smoldering remains of the faithful boat slipped beneath the surface of the sea.

Bartimaeus and Leif proceeded along the well-beaten road through the Dark Wood. The limbs of the trees on either side stretched across the road forming a canopy that blocked much of the sun. The ambush came so suddenly that the pair of Volcanadians had no time to think. All at once, the path ahead was blocked by three men on horseback and half a dozen men on foot emerged from the undergrowth and encircled them from behind. These men were not Alfabetian, but rather seemed to be a band of thieves. Regardless of who they were, they did not appear friendly in the least.

"Drop your weapons" shouted one of the men on horseback.

Leif said nothing. He chose to respond with his flare-launcher. He fired the weapon at the speaker, shooting the man backward out of the saddle. Leif and Bartimaeus charged into the woods to their left heading due west away from the trail. The thieves gave chase while firing arrows at the fleeing pair. Leif was concentrating on avoiding tree branches that threatened to sweep him out of the saddle when he heard Bartimaeus emit a peculiar groan. He turned just in time to witness his companion go toppling off of his unihorn, an arrow protruding from his back.

"Bartimaeus!" Leif cried. He hauled back on the reigns of his mount and jumped off so he could run to his friend's side. "Barty? Barty wake up." Leif said, his eyes searching desperately for signs of life. Bartimaeus's face was deathly pale and his breathing was shallow. The arrow had struck him just below his right shoulder-blade and the wound was just starting to bleed out around the shaft. Leif's hands shook uncontrollably, and he was unsure of what to do. He was brought back to his senses by another arrow that struck the tree beside him. Realizing their pursuers would be upon them in moments, he broke the shaft off just above the wound and heaved the smaller boy up onto his shoulder. Then he turned away from the pursuing thieves and took off at a lope through the dense forest. His adrenaline intensified his natural brute-strength and made him nearly unstoppable as he crashed through the brush. He burst through some trees into a small clearing and nearly ran off the edge of a ravine. He teetered for a second on the edge of the precipice and looked down at a rushing river far below. He shifted the weight on his shoulder and Bartimaeus let out a pitiful groan. Leif searched desperately for a new path to take or a place to hide. The ravine was far too wide to jump across, even without the load he was carrying. He turned to head back into the trees and saw to his dismay that one of the mounted bushwhackers had just arrived in the clearing. The man's face broke into a leering grin as he raised a crossbow to his shoulder. There was nowhere else to turn, no other option, so Leif stepped off the edge and plummeted to the raging waters at the bottom of the canyon.

Chapter 12

Mission Reassessment

An hour after we abandoned ship, Joanna and I found ourselves creeping through the scrub grass as we tried to get closer to the pirate camp. We had made it to shore and gone inland, soggy, but none the worse for wear. The problem we now faced was obtaining a new mode of transportation; and the pirates seemed to have the only boats for miles around. The cove from which the corsair vessels had emerged seemed to be their home base. The beach was covered with all manner of boats that had most likely been, shall we say, "repossessed." A collection of shanties and ramshackle shacks made up the living quarters for the community of thieves. With all the vessels strewn about it would be easy to find a replacement for the one we had lost. The difficult part would be getting out of the cove alive.

"I like… that one!" Joanna said, pointing out a particular craft.

"It's all yours" I said. "Just as soon as you figure out a plan to get away with it."

Joanna smiled slyly. "What makes you think I don't already have one?"

As Leif started to regain his senses, he heard the babble of water flowing nearby. "Water?.. He had jumped into the water hadn't he?.. Him and Bartimaeus… And Bartimaeus was hurt… But where was he now?"

He opened his eyes and lifted his head slightly. He had a throbbing pain in his head and his vision was a bit out of focus. He found that he was lying face down on a stretch of gravel with his legs still resting in the shallow water of the riverbank. He had no idea how far the river had carried him, but it must have been a fair distance because the cliff he had jumped from was nowhere in sight. He let his head back down to ease the throbbing… and then he heard something… the sound of footsteps approaching. Without looking up, he discreetly pulled a dagger from his belt with his left hand. As the unknown person drew closer, Leif suddenly jumped to a crouched position with his dagger held before him. The pain in his head deepened because of the sudden movement and he struggled to keep his balance. The person who had approached was not at all what he had expected. Standing before him was a girl who appeared to be about his own age. She was small, barefoot, wearing a dress made of animal skins, and had thick blond hair adorned with beads and bird feathers. The two stared at each other for a moment without saying anything. When Leif attempted to speak, he found that his throat was so hoarse that he could do little more than grunt. He was just about to try standing up when the girl suddenly started twirling a leather strap with some sort of ball attached to the end. Before he knew what was happening, the ball and strap flew from her hand and struck him right between the eyes. Leif fell over backwards into the shallow water and his vision clouded until there was nothing but darkness.

Raucous laughter filled the pirate camp as they drank to excess and devoured their dinner of fresh roasted meat. Night was beginning to fall, and all seemed well until one of the more-sober men cried out with alarm. Several of the boats on the beach were going up in flames and one of the larger vessels was making a run for the mouth of the cove. Ignoring the fires, the pirates swarmed onto their warship and ran out the sweeps to give chase. None of the brigands noticed as they shoved off that a smaller craft was tied to the stern of their ship being towed along behind. The pirates reached the mouth of the cove and continued out into the open sea in pursuit of their quarry. Joanna severed the tow line on the front of her new boat and glided to a stop just outside the cove. Jairus swam up on the port side.

"Permission to come aboard?" He requested jokingly.

"Granted" Joanna said with a smile as she helped to pull him up over the side. Jairus had been aboard the decoy craft that the pirates were chasing and had slipped over the side after leaving the cove. The pirates would eventually outpace their quarry only to find that the vessel had no one aboard. In the meantime, Jairus and Joanna would resume their quest aboard their new craft.

"A brilliant plan milady" Jairus said with a flourishing bow.

"Why thank you good sir" she responded with a mocking attempt at a curtsy. The two of them laughed as they went about setting the sail and getting underway. Valuable time had been lost today, but hopefully it would be made up tomorrow. "I hope Leif and Bartimaeus are making good time" Jairus said. And Joanna nodded her agreement.

Leif awoke to the tingling sensation that made him feel he was falling or swinging. He looked around and realized that he was indeed suspended above the ground. He hung in the air by two ropes, one at his hips and the other around his chest. Additional ropes tied to four different trees held his arms and legs outstretched. The swinging motion was being caused by a small boy who was nudging him with a stick. The boy was probably eight or nine, had dark hair, and was clothed only in a dirty pair of animal-skin britches.

"Hey! Hey! Stop that. Get away from me." Leif shouted. The boy dropped the stick and ran away down a nearby path. Leif heard a giggle off to his left and turned to see who was there. Leaning with her back up against a tree was the girl that had knocked him out.

"Oh, it's you" he said disgustedly.

"It's nice to see you too" she responded with sarcasm and a smile. "How's your head?" she asked and proceeded to walk over to see for herself.

"Still holding together, despite you're trying to kill me" Leif replied.

The girl laughed again and moved to stand directly beneath him so she could look up into his face. "If I wanted you dead, you would be" she said simply.

Leif stared down into her rebellious blue eyes and saw the truth in her statement.

"How about letting me down from here?" Leif asked.

"Why should I? She responded.

"Why not?" He countered.

"I asked you first" she said matter-of-factly.

Leif sighed, closed his eyes, and took a deep breath in an attempt to stem the tension building within him. "Will you please let me down?" He asked politely.

The girl mimicked his sigh, took a deep breath, and said "Why should I?"

"You are infuriating" Leif said in exasperation.

"Yeah, I hear that a lot" she said. And then she turned and walked off down the trail.

"Hey! Wait! LET ME DOWN!" He thundered.

Chapter 13

An Interesting Turn of Events

Jairus was exhausted. He and Joanna had taken turns at the tiller through the night, so each had managed to get a few hours of sleep. Even so, the strain of the last few days combined with the lack of a full night's rest was beginning to show. It appeared that things were only going to get worse. A massive storm was building right over the top of them. Colossal thunderheads were forming into a single mass of blackness with white streaks of lightning cutting across the sky. If conditions got too bad they might have to go ashore.

"I don't like the look of this weather" Joanna said, voicing the concern that plagued both of their minds.

"Neither do I" he responded, "but we have to keep going. If we maintain this pace, we could be landed on the outskirts of Layatreb by tomorrow morning."

"Well we won't do anybody any good if we drown" she observed.

Jairus ignored her, though he knew she was absolutely correct. Whether they reached Enos in time or not, nobody would gain from their dying at sea. They sailed along at top speed for nearly another hour before conditions started to get dangerous. The wind was gusting so badly that it threatened to rip the sails.

The waves were becoming much bigger and more ferocious. Joanna took over at the tiller and Jairus fought to keep their craft from becoming swamped. Things were getting worse all the time, so Jairus finally signaled for Joanna to steer for the beach. As soon as the boat scraped up on shore, they gathered their few supplies and jumped overboard into the surf. As they plodded up to higher ground, Joanna called out to Jairus: "Are we going to take cover and wait it out or just keep moving?"

"I think we better proceed on foot" he replied. "We can't afford to lose any more time." A bolt of lightning flashed across the sky illuminating the beach as the two weary youths continued on through the deluge.

Leif looked up at the sound of voices approaching. Three men came trudging up the trail with the obnoxious little blond following close behind. Two of the men stopped and crossed their arms intimidatingly as the third walked right up to Leif. Despite the fact that he hung suspended nearly six feet off the ground, Leif found that he still had to look up to meet the glaring eyes of the towering man. The gentleman had thick blond hair tinged with gray that came down to his shoulders and a matching goatee on his weathered face. His shirtless torso was swathed with numerous scars, some older, some newer. All he wore was a pair of buckskin britches, leather moccasins, and a belt that held a hefty dirk in a scabbard.

"What do you want here?" the big man growled in a deep drawling voice.

"Right now, what I *"want"* is to be let down" Leif replied evenly.

"You threatened my daughter" the man said, pointing to the girl.

"I didn't mean too" Leif countered defensively. "I was just trying to defend myself, and then she thumped me in the face!"

The man glanced at his daughter "Ya should've hit him harder" he said, to which she responded with a smirk. Turning back to Leif, the man said: "The fact remains that you pulled a knife on my baby girl. As if it wasn't bad enough that you were trespassing on my land."

"I fell into a river" Leif explained. "I had no intention of trespassing. I didn't even know this land belonged to anyone."

"Boy, this is Trog land" the man stated.

"Trog?" Leif asked with confusion.

"The Troglodotians" the man clarified. They are my people, I am their chief, and this is our land; trespassers aren't welcome.

"Well chief, if you can see fit to cut me down I'll be on my way" offered Leif.

"You're not going anywhere until I say so, if you go at all."

"Can I make a different request then?" Leif pleaded.

"You can 'request' anything you want, that don't mean it's gonna happen" the chieftain replied.

"There was another boy in the river with me" Leif explained. "My friend Bartimaeus… He was wounded… An arrow in the back… Did your people find him?"

"Another trespasser?" The Chief said with disgust.

"We weren't trespassing, we were running for our lives!" Leif yelled, his muscles rippling as he strained against his bonds. "And it was my fault" he continued. "Bartimaeus tried to convince me to take another route. We were on a mission for our king and I was trying to save time." His voice trailed off and his eyes began to well up. "I made the decision to move ahead and Bartimaeus got shot. It was my fault… And now he is probably dead. Leif let his body go limp against the ropes. His soul was consumed with feelings of guilt, failure, grief, and despair. He couldn't even retain his dignity by shielding his tears from this group of strangers. He didn't really care when he felt his bonds being cut loose. He just let himself fall facedown into the dirt. As he laid there, he felt his oversized, work-hardened hand being gripped, firmly but gently, by a softer hand that was much smaller than his own. "Come with me" the girl whispered softly, "and I will take you to Bartimaeus.

Chapter 14

Unexpected Allies

Jairus and Joanna were both exhausted as they trudged on through the pouring rain. It became obvious that they needed some form of shelter, so they headed for a nearby stand of trees. As they reached the tree line, Joanna tugged Jairus' sleeve to draw his attention to a light that shined in the distance. They moved quickly towards the source in hopes that the owner was somebody friendly. They found themselves standing outside a small cabin with the glow of firelight shining through the window. Joanna drew her dagger and stood to one side of the entrance as Jairus knocked on the door. After a moment, a young man opened the door and peered out to see who was there.

"For crying out loud! The man exclaimed. What are you doing out on a night like this? Get inside before you drown. Jairus entered the cabin with Joanna following behind and the young man closed the door to the storm.

"Of all the nights to go gallivanting through the hills, you two picked tonight?

Jairus more or less ignored the man and his boisterous conversation. He was too busy scanning their new surroundings looking for potential threats. There were five other men of various ages lounging in the small but comfortable interior of the cabin. All of them seemed equally surprised, but not otherwise bothered at the intrusion from the two Volcanadians. It was a warm and cheerful atmosphere, and something that smelled delicious was cooking in the hearth. Jairus looked at Joanna and saw a frightened look in her eyes. Following her gaze, he spotted a half-dozen cloaks hanging in the corner, each of them bearing the insignia of the Layatrebian military.

Jairus tensed up and shifted his gaze back to Joanna. Jairus wasn't the only one looking her way. In fact, every man in the room was giving her their undivided attention. She may have been cold, tired, and dripping on the floor, but in the light from the fireplace her appearance was quite stunning.

"I am called Marek" said the gentleman that had let them in. "Who might you be?" He asked. Joanna introduced Jairus and then herself to the Layatrebians.

"Welcome to our humble abode" Marek said with a sweep of his arm.

"Thank you" said Jairus. "We didn't want to intrude, but the weather was getting pretty fierce."

"No intrusion at all" said Marek. "You both are Volcanadians right?"

Once again, Jairus and Joanna exchanged looks of alarm. Marek seemed to take notice of this and raised one eyebrow quizzically.

"Yes, we are" Joanna acknowledged.

"My grandmother was Volcanadian" Marek offered with friendly smile.

"That's nice" Joanna responded uncertainly

"So, what are you doing out here?" asked one of the other soldiers.

Jairus replied with a half-truth. "We're going to meet my father near Layatreb" he said. "We were traveling by boat and the storm ran us aground." This explanation seemed more than satisfactory to the men.

"So, what brings all of you way out here?" Jairus asked in an attempt to shift the conversation away from Joanna and himself.

"A team of woodcutters are felling trees not far from here" Marek explained. "Bands of thieves tend to prowl this area, so we were sent out to provide a little protection.

It occurred to Jairus that these men were either incredibly good actors or they were completely oblivious to Rotiart's betrayal of Volcanadas.

"We're heading back to Layatreb tomorrow and you're welcome to ride along with us" Marek offered.

"No!" Joanna and Jairus replied in unison, both a little too loudly and also too quickly.

"All right you two" said Marek firmly. "You're too jumpy and suspicious to just be wayward travelers. What's going on that you haven't told us?

"We're running away to get married" Joanna blurted out after a tense silence.

Marek's face softened slightly. "Well now, that is… adorable… and beautiful… and a LIE! And do you know how I know that it's a lie? Because all the color went out of Jairus' face when you said it and I think he may pass out."

Marek looked at both of them sternly. "Tell me the truth" he ordered. "Forget it… we're leaving" Jairus stated. He made a move for the door only to be blocked by Marek. Jairus drew his short launcher and Joanna followed suit. The Layatrebians all jumped to their feet with weapons in hand.

"What's going on?" Marek asked angrily. "You dare to draw weapons against us. We're supposed to be allies."

"Tell that to your king" Joanna said.

Marek's eyes narrowed. "Would you care to elaborate on that?"

Over the next hour, Jairus and Joanna took turns relating the events that had taken place over the last three days. At the end of the hour, six somber-faced Layatrebians sat around a table in disbelief.

"It's no wonder that you were so nervous when you got here" Marek said.

"So, what are we supposed to do?" asked one of the soldiers. "We have pledged our allegiance to our King, and now we sit here drinking tea with two people he has branded as enemies."

"True" said Marek. "But I don't feel compelled to honor my pledge when my King will not honor his own. I can't speak for the rest of you, but tomorrow I am riding with Jairus and Joanna to warn their king. If that is treason, then so be it."

Marek's comrades nodded their agreement. "Now" he said, "we need to get these two some dry clothes and a place to sleep."

Marek gave a change of his own clothes to Jairus who accepted them gratefully. One of the other Layatrebians, a man of very slight build, was good enough to share a suit of clothes with Joanna. A pallet was made near the fireplace for Jairus to sleep on and Joanna was given a bed in the cabin's loft. As if all this kindness wasn't enough, Marek insisted that two Volcanadians have a share of the stew that had been cooking on the fire. After they had eaten, all the inhabitants of the cabin went to bed. But Jairus just couldn't sleep. He couldn't stop thinking about the importance of getting word to Lord Enos. Marek's voice drifted over from the cot by the door,

"strange isn't it?"

Jairus sat up part way, "what's strange?"

"That after all these years of being allies, our nations are at odds because of one man's greed" Marek said in disbelief.

"It's crazy" Jairus stated, "but I guess that is what greed does to people." Both young men fell silent and gradually receded to a state of fitful slumber.

Chapter 15

A Duel of Honor

The girl dragged Leif down the trail as if she was leading a mule by the nose. He just followed obediently as she led him to a path that descended into a wide canyon. Leif was somewhat surprised to see that the canyon walls rising up on either side of him were bustling with activity. Dozens of cave openings pitted the face of the stone, connected by carved-out pathways and wooden catwalks. Spanning the canyon at certain intervals were rope bridges that connected one side to the other. Children splashed and played in the river on the canyon floor. Adults tended to cook-fires, hung laundry, and sharpened tools. The Troglodotian settlement was comparable to any other village or city of its size. The only major difference seemed to be that much of the community appeared to have been built in caves or underground. They continued walking through the canyon drawing curious stares from everyone they passed. They stepped up onto a wooden platform and the girl pulled a lever releasing some sort of counterweight that hoisted the platform into the air.

The lift stopped at the entrance to a large cavern and the two of them went inside. As they entered, a dark form whooshed over Leif's head sending him flat on the ground.

"What was that!? Leif cried. "You've never seen a banther?" The girl asked.

"A banther? No, I haven't." he responded.

She stepped back out of the cave and gave a low whistle. Within seconds, the creature reappeared and landed at her side.

"A panther with bat wings" Leif observed, "A banther. That's

A banther of the Troglodotian caverns

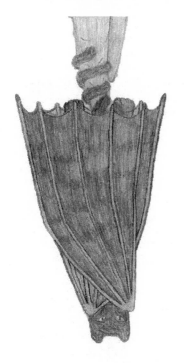

remarkable" He stated. "

Wait until you see this" she said. Reentering the cave, she grabbed a torch from a sconce on the wall and gestured with it to the high ceiling of the cavern. Leif looked up and saw with amazement that scores of the cat-like creatures were hanging in the cave amongst jagged outcroppings and stalactites.

"Come on" the girl urged. Leif followed her down a corridor to another part of the cave. They arrived in a room that obviously served as living quarters and Leif was overjoyed to see Bartimaeus lying on a bed.

"Leif, you're alive!" Bartimaeus called out weakly. "Forget me, how are you?" Leif asked with concern. Bartimaeus was still quite pale and he had a large cloth bandage wrapped clear around his chest.

"I'm fine, or at least as well as can be expected. I only woke up a little while ago."

"I was afraid you were dead" said Leif gravely. "That arrow went deep, and you look as though you have lost a lot of blood."

Bartimaeus nodded. "That's what I was told. But Attimara says they got the arrowhead out alright, and they applied a salve that should prevent festering."

"Who is Attimara?" Leif asked curiously.

"She's the girl that just brought you in" explained Bartimaeus. Leif turned and saw that the girl, "Attimara," had slipped out and left them alone.

"She's nice" said Bartimaeus.

"She's something" Leif countered.

Bartimaeus ignored this remark and looked at Leif seriously.

"I don't even know what day it is" he said. "Are we too late to catch Enos before he reaches Layatreb?"

Leif sighed dejectedly, "even if I were to leave right now and travel all night, I couldn't reach the army before the fighting starts."

Attimara came back in carrying a tray covered with food. She set a platter before Leif that held eight thick slices of roasted venison, half of a roast chicken, three pan-fried trout, and an entire loaf of fresh baked bread.

"I thought you might be a little hungry after hanging around all day" she said good-humoredly.

"Do I get food?" Bartimaeus asked forlornly. "No real food yet" she responded firmly. "For right now, I've got a thick broth to help you get your strength back. And I'll feed it to you while you both tell me more about this mission you were supposed to be on."

Leif and Bartimaeus took turns eating and storytelling until Attimara was up to date and they had eaten their fill. She was fascinated with their story and impassioned by their fervent loyalty to their people and their leader.

"So that's it" Leif surmised. "By this time tomorrow, our army may very well have been decimated and then our kingdom is next."

Attimara was quiet for a moment, then she jumped to her feet with a fire in her eyes and headed out of the cave.

"Wait here" she ordered. Less than an hour later, two Trog men entered the cave bearing a stretcher on which to carry Bartimaeus and a third man came to escort Leif. They were brought outside and lowered to the canyon floor by means of the lift. Then, they moved a short distance up the canyon to a large gathering of people. Hundreds of Troglodotians filled a sort of natural open-air meeting hall. At the center of the mass was a raised platform, and resting on top, a throne constructed of bones, antlers, and animal hides; seated here of course was Attimara's father. As Leif and Bartimaeus were brought forward, the chieftain stood, raised his hands and a hush fell over the crowd.

"I am Atticus, Chief of the Trog."

"TROG!" the people shouted in unison.

The Chieftain stared hard at the Volcanadians as he continued. "My daughter Attimara has told us about the mess your people have gotten into and she has suggested that the Trog step in to help you out. What *I* would like *you* to do," he said pointing at

Leif, "is explain to us why I should ask my people to fight a battle that isn't ours, to save people we don't even know."

Leif took a deep breath and stepped forward. "I am Leif, the son of Liras. I am a warrior of Volcanadas. My people march to answer a plea for help, not knowing that it is a plot to destroy us. If the plot is carried out and Volcanadas falls, it will only be a matter of time before Eleminos turns his attention to the Trog. If you choose to help us, a bond can be formed between our two nations. We can become allies and hold strong against those who threaten us."

"You're just a soldier, and a young one at that" Atticus stated. "Why should I believe your people will form an alliance with the Trog just because you say so?

"Without the help of the Trog, my people will die tomorrow." Leif said bluntly. "The very existence of my people rests in your hands."

The chief nodded as he considered this. "There's just one more thing I'd like to ask" he said. "Before I agree to fight alongside of somebody, I wanna know what they're capable of. Are you volcano people any good in a fight?"

"Some say we're the best" Leif answered proudly.

Atticus scoffed at this. "I'll believe that when I see it. How about a demonstration?"

"What kind of demonstration?" Leif asked warily.

"A one on one contest, you against our best, first man cornered is the loser" said Atticus.

Leif nodded his agreement to these terms and a murmur of excitement rippled through the crowd. Attimara appeared at Leif's side with his sword in hand. "Good luck" she whispered.

"Who am I fighting?" Leif whispered back.

Attimara's eyes rolled back to her father's throne. Atticus had stood up from his chair and taken up a heavy double-bladed battleax. Leif felt a slight flutter in his stomach as he realized who his opponent would be.

"I'm ready when you are" the hulking chieftain called out.

Leif took a deep breath, drew his sword, and charged forward to start the contest. Atticus lunged off the platform to meet the boy's advance and swung his battleax. The weapons collided with a resounding clash and

The battleax of Chief Atticus

the people erupted with cheers for their chief. Leif found himself struggling to meet the onslaught of heavy blows from the older man. Despite the Trog's somewhat advanced age, he was surprisingly quick and agile. Leif counterattacked with his best combinations of cuts and slashes only to be continually driven back by Atticus's advance.

"Time to try something different" Leif thought to himself.

Atticus swung his ax in a vertical cut and Leif raised his blade to meet it. But instead of absorbing the force of the blow, Leif allowed himself to collapse beneath it. He dropped to the ground, laying on his back in front of the chieftain, and kicked upward with both legs as hard as he could. The blow struck Atticus in his lower abdomen and he fell over backwards gasping for breath. Leif rolled to his feet and swung his sword as the chief attempted to rise. Atticus ducked beneath the oncoming blade and swung his own weapon, hitting Leif with the full force of the flat side of the ax-head. Leif was thrown through the air by the force of the blow and tumbled across the ground until he rolled to a stop at Bartimaeus' feet.

"Get up" Bartimaeus yelled over the roar of the crowd.

Leif lurched to his feet and retrieved his fallen weapon just in time to meet a fresh attack from the Trog. The fight dragged on for several minutes more with each of the contestants giving as good as they got. The crowd fell silent as they watched the level of mastery displayed by the veteran soldier and the young neophyte. The duel was brought to an end by Atticus, more or less by accident. An underhand swing of his battleax hooked Leif's sword in such a way that it was torn from his grasp. Just like that, the contest was over, and Leif bowed his head in acceptance of his defeat.

Atticus took a moment to catch his breath and returned to his platform. Standing in front of his throne, he turned to address the crowd.

"People of the Trog. This boy has fought well today. I expect that one day he will be a greater warrior, even than myself. If his people fight with half the spirit and determination that he has, then I would be proud to stand and fight with them. Any of you who feel the same way should say so now."

Slowly at first, but with growing intensity, the Troglodotians began drawing their weapons and raising them in the air to indicate their willingness to fight. As more and more blades were lifted toward the heavens, the crowds began cheering once again. Atticus raised his booming voice, so he could be heard over the ruckus. "Pack up, we leave tonight."

Chapter 16

In Defense of the King

Jairus and Joanna rode double on a borrowed horse in a group with Marek and his companions. They had left the cabin in the woods before dawn in hopes of finally catching up to Enos. They had reached the tail end of the Volcanadian convoy a few miles from Layatreb and picked up the pace to reach the head of the procession. On arrival, Jairus scanned the mounted figures leading the party in hope of spotting Lord Enos or General Jabirus. His searching eyes fell on Eber and he spurred his horse in the direction of his uncle the Prince.

"Eber!" Jairus called out. The prince turned in the saddle at the sound of his name and seemed quite surprised when he saw who it was that had called to him.

"Jairus? What on earth are you doing here?" He asked in astonishment.

"Eber, I must speak to the King?" Jairus said urgently. "Where is he?"

"What's wrong" Eber asked with concern.

"WHERE EBER? WHERE?" Jairus shouted impatiently.

Eber pointed across the valley towards the distant city of Layatreb. "The King, your father, and several others just rode ahead to meet with Rotiart" Eber explained. Jairus paled at the impending doom of his King and his father.

"CAVALRY ADVANCE!" he hollered at the top of his lungs.

"THE KING IS IN DANGER!"

All of the mounted Volcanadians surged ahead at the cry of warning. Joanna slid off of the horse to lighten its load and Jairus kicked it to a gallop in the direction of the city. Marek and his fellow Layatrebians followed at his heels.

Joanna stood alone at the head of the army as every mounted Volcanadian rushed to protect their leader. A lieutenant in charge of a detachment of foot-soldiers rushed up to her side. His name was Boaz, he was young, not much older than she herself, and was clearly frazzled by the sudden turn of events.

"What is going on? He asked.

"Rotiart betrayed us" she explained. "He conspired with Eleminos to lead us into a trap. The Alfabetian forces could attack us at any time."

"So, what should we do? Boaz inquired.

"You're asking me?" Joanna asked skeptically.

"Why not?" he responded. "My superiors are a bit busy at the moment and you seem to have a better grasp of the situation anyway."

Joanna considered this and looked around to determine what their best option was.

"Have the convoy move to the coast as fast as possible" she ordered. "When we get there, we'll line up the wagons for makeshift defenses."

Jairus's horse was blowing hard as they crossed the valley. The poor beast had already traveled many miles today carrying two people and this unexpected gallop was poor thanks. Still, the situation was dire and Jairus pushed for more speed. "Lord please let me get there in time."

Up ahead, Enos and the seven men with him had already reached the main gates of Layatreb. As they approached the gate it remained closed and Rotiart himself appeared at the wall overhead. Jabirus felt himself tensing up. The odd reception didn't set well in his mind and he began watching carefully for signs of trouble.

"Greetings friend. We came as fast as we could" Enos shouted upward.

"So I see" Rotiart replied smugly. "The magnificent King Enos of Volcanadas rushed at my call. Always faithful and true to your word… And it has cost you your life!" Rotiart raised his arm and a dozen archers appeared at the wall. Jabirus dove from his saddle, swept Enos to the ground, and covered him with his own body as shafts of death hailed down from the archers above.

Jairus saw the arrows raining down on the Volcanadians and feared that they were too late. He and the six Layatrebians had pulled far ahead of the Volcanadian unihorns and reached the gate with a decent lead. Marek and his friends shouted and waved at the men on the wall to hold their fire. The archers were confused to see Layatrebians down below and momentarily stayed their bows. This pause was long enough for the Volcanadian marksmen to get within range and the fury of their flare-launchers swept the battlements of Layatreb. Jairus rode his mount directly to the victims of Rotiart's ambush and was horrified by the sight that met his eyes. Several of Enos's companions had been hit, but the one that drew Jairus' undivided attention was the form of General Jabirus lying in a pool of blood.

Chapter 17

A Noble Sacrifice

Seeing his father like this made Jairus yearn for the blood of those responsible. No stronger bond existed between a father and son than that which the two of them shared. His vision blurred with tears as he knelt by his father's side. And then, to his surprise, Jabirus sat up and turned to face him. It was then that he realized, the puddle of blood that soaked the ground had not come from his father, it was from Lord Enos.

"Help me carry him" Jabirus sobbed. And the two of them picked up their fallen king. Marek and his comrades helped collect the rest of the wounded and they turned to flee Layatreb under the cover of the Volcanadian launcher-fire.

They stopped in the valley when they got out of range of Layatreb's archers and laid the king in the grass. Eber came forward to bid a heartrending farewell to his father.

"I tried to save him" Jabirus said weakly. "I tried to use myself to shield him, but he rolled over on top of me."

"That's just like my father" Eber said with a tearful smile. "He knew you would gladly die for him… Doing the same for you was just his character." He leaned down and embraced the noble warrior. Then he stood up, drew his father's sword, and turned to mount his unihorn. "Come" he commanded. "There will be time for mourning later. Rotiart has betrayed us, and for that he must pay, but this too must wait. What do we know of the Alfabetian attack?"

"Very little" Jairus answered. "A portion of their army has Volcanadas under siege; they attacked the day after you left. Eleminos was supposed to pin our forces down in front of Layatreb so we would have nowhere to run."

"How did you get here?" Jabirus asked, just now realizing that his son was there.

"Eros sent four of us to try to warn Enos." Jairus explained. "I came most of the way by sea accompanied by the daughter of General Johannes." Jairus turned to the six friendly Layatrebians and introduced Marek and his friends. "We met them yesterday, and they helped us get the rest of the way here." Jairus turned back to Eber. "I'm so sorry that we didn't get here in time."

Eber looked down at him and smiled sadly. "You did everything you could… And the King would be proud."

Joanna had ordered that the wagons be formed into two half-circles and had the men start digging earthen breastworks to extend them. With the defenses in this configuration, a frontal attack from Eleminos's army would be somewhat divided. This might in turn create an opening in the enemy's offensive line that could be penetrated by the Volcanadian cavalry. Joanna herself was helping to unload extra ammunition from the wagons when she saw Jairus returning with the army's mounted forces. She rushed over to meet them and knew from the solemn looks on everybody's faces the tragedy that had befallen their people. Her suspicion was confirmed when she saw the body of Enos draped across the back of a unihorn. Her heart ached as she realized that they had failed to save him.

The Prince road up and observed the soldiers as they worked. "Well done setting up these defenses" praised Eber. "But I want trenches dug along the barricades for additional reinforcement. I also want patrols formed immediately to find out exactly where the Alfabetians are.

All nearby trees of manageable size were cut down to be used in the fortifications. Raiding parties were sent out to the farms in the surrounding countryside to collect additional materials. Eber didn't want any of the civilians to be harmed and only those possessions useful to the defense were taken. Wagons, carts, barrels, and more were hauled back and added to the makeshift barriers. Within a few short hours of their arrival at Layatreb, the Volcanadian compliment had established modest, yet highly defensible fortifications. There wasn't much left to do besides wait. Alfabetian forces had been spotted amassing in the woods to the south and west. The assault would likely begin at dusk so the attackers could advance with the sun at their backs. Warships from Layatreb had been put to sea and were anchored off the coast awaiting the attack. The Volcanadians were growing tense as they awaited the forthcoming battle.

Jairus himself had begun to create a rut in the ground from pacing back and forth at his post. Joanna approached him with two cups of cold tea, his with extra sugar, the way he liked it best. He nodded his thanks as he took the cup and resumed his pacing.

"How are you doing?" She asked as he strode back and forth.

"I'm fine" he replied. "I just can't stand the waiting."

"Not about that, I meant about losing your grandfather" she corrected.

Jairus was quiet for a moment. "I feel guilty" he said finally. "Just a few minutes earlier and I could have saved him." He shook his head bitterly and turned his back to her.

Joanna stepped towards him and placed a hand on his shoulder. "He wouldn't want you to feel guilty" she said tenderly. "He would want you to pick yourself up, dust yourself off, and be proud that you had the courage to try. You can't let this eat you up. A tragedy can tear your life apart if you let it, but it can also make you stronger."

Jairus took a deep breath and turned to look at her with an appreciative smile.

"How'd you get to be so smart?" He inquired flippantly.

Joanna was about to make a sarcastic reply when she was interrupted by a call of alarm from a sentry. She and Jairus squinted against the setting sun in the western sky and saw Alfabetian infantrymen pouring out of the woods. It was starting. The windswept plains that rested before the city of Layatreb would soon be stained crimson with the blood of fallen warriors.

Chapter 18

A Gruesome Affair

Jairus and Joanna ran to the center of the northern barricade were Jabirus was barking orders.

"Jairus! I want you to grab some extra ammunition and man the barricade. Joanna! You go with this group down to the beach. We need our sharpshooters to hold off the Layatrebian landing parties." The two friends wished each other good luck and turned to the assignments they had been given.

Joanna armed herself with two regular launchers, four short ones, and ammunition from the army's supplies before running down to the beach with about thirty others. She picked out a spot nestled behind some boulders and laid her armaments within easy reach. The enemy ships were not yet moving to shore. They would most likely wait until the battle with the Alfabetians had the Volcanadians fully occupied. "Lord, I ask for a sharp eye and a steady hand" she prayed.

Jairus found himself positioned next to Marek at the barricade. This surprised him because the other friendly Layatrebians had taken leave to avoid the conflict.

"Are you sure you want to stick around?" Jairus asked. "We are fighting your people."

"You're fighting my people, *I* am fighting the Alfabetians" Marek said with a grin.

The enemy infantry was not moving too quickly but maintained a steady march. As they drew closer to the range of the flare-launchers, the first line of Eleminos's soldiers raised shields to protect themselves. The shields were long rectangular planks of hard wood covered with a thin sheet of metal. A soldier carrying such a shield had protection for nearly his entire body. These shields were awkward and heavy but were a sufficient barrier to long-range fire from bows and launchers alike. The Alfabetians walked in a line, shoulder-to-shoulder, with their shields overlapped to create a wall. This moving wall afforded protection for all of the infantrymen concealed behind it. There was precious little the Volcanadians could do to stop the enemy advance.

The distance between the opposing forces was diminishing quickly and the Alfabetians had continued to advance unchecked, but this was about to change. Jabirus had come up with the idea of planting bundles of excess ammunition in the tall grass of the battlefield. Each bundle would serve as an explosive package and would be detonated by a shot from a Volcanadian sharpshooter. When the Alfabetian wall reached the line of explosives, fifteen flare-launchers fired at once setting off fifteen corresponding explosions. The shock from the blasts knocked many of the shield carriers off their feet. This created gaps in their protective wall which meant the Volcanadians now had something to shoot at.

"FIRE AT WILL!" Eber ordered.

The opposing infantry surged forward against the volleys of fire from the Volcanadian defenders.

Joanna jumped at the sound of the shooting and explosions. She couldn't see the battlefield from her spot in the rocks, but she could definitely hear it.

"They're running out the sweeps!" announced a soldier off to her left. She whipped her head around and saw that the warships were indeed headed to shore. She took a deep breath to ease her racing heart and checked the loads in her launchers for the fifth time.

Marek abandoned the launcher he had borrowed so he could repel the attackers trying to climb the barricade. He did so by flailing madly with his chosen weapon, a mace-and-chain with a heavy spiked ball. Marek's defense left Jairus free to load and fire his launcher as fast as he could without interruption. Despite their best efforts, and those of their comrades, the enemy forces were beginning to overwhelm them. As Jairus was taking aim to fire once again, he heard three sharp blasts of a horn signaling the Volcanadian cavalry to charge. The cavalry had been divided into three groups commanded by Jabirus, Johannes, and Eber. Like the outstretched claws of a giant crustacean, the two generals led their troops to the north and south respectively in a sweeping pincer movement. Eber led his command straight up the middle of the battlefield from between the arched fortifications. The unihorn mounted Volcanadians plowed into the ranks of the Alfabetian infantry, wreaking havoc with blade and bludgeon.

The first warship had a significant lead on the other three as it scraped through the shallows to the edge of the beach. A great door on the front of the vessel dropped open and splashed into the surf forming a ramp. Layatrebian soldiers poured out of the ship with swords drawn and shields raised. The first one to set foot on the sand dropped dead with the head of a flarefly through his throat. Joanna quickly reloaded and fired again. The concentrated fire from Joanna and the other defenders cut down most of the disembarking soldiers, but a few of them still managed to make it across the beach. Five Volcanadians were forced to drop their launchers and fight hand to hand. The skirmish was quickly finished and the good prevailed, but the fight was far from over. The next two ships would land simultaneously with the last one close behind. There was no way these thirty defenders could hold off so many and there would be no help from the main force of Volcanadians. "Lord God, we need help" Joanna prayed aloud.

The enemy soldiers were falling back from the barricades to engage the Volcanadian cavalry. Jairus and the other defenders climbed over their fortifications and went out onto the battlefield in pursuit. Jairus waded into the thick of the battle with Marek watching his back. They moved from adversary to adversary engaging them and overcoming them. The Alfabetians were being driven steadily backward from whence they came. From his position in the field of battle, it almost seemed to Jairus that they were winning. He dispatched the foe that was currently trying to shiv him and stopped to catch his breath and evaluate his surroundings. He looked to the west and his heart fell. Five reinforcement companies of infantry were just reaching the edge of the conflict. In addition, four units of Alfabetian cavalry were at the edge of the woods preparing to charge. As if that wasn't bad enough, a force of Layatrebian cavalry was forming at the gate of the city. The Volcanadians had done all they could, but the number of enemies was just too great.

Chapter 19

From the Jaws of Despair

Joanna heard a gasping groan off to her right and was horrified to see one of her comrades dropping to the ground clutching a mortal wound. The poor man had been struck in the chest by a bolt from a crossbow. She dropped behind her rock for cover, and not a moment too soon, as she both felt and heard the hiss of another bolt flying dangerously close to her position. She looked over the rock and saw that at least two archers were positioned in the crow's-nest of the first warship.

"Great" she thought, "We're already outnumbered and now we are being picked off one by one." She would have to keep an eye on the archers above, but most of her attention had to be focused on the landing parties. The next two warships scraped onto the shore and dropped open their ramps. Layatrebians flooded towards the beach with more than twice the force of the first vessel. Ten enemy soldiers were headed directly to Joanna's position. She fired her launcher and then discarded it, knowing there would be no more time for reloads. She snatched up two of her short launchers and fired. Two more of the foes fell. Then she picked up her last two launchers and charged to meet the attack. She fired both launchers and killed one more soldier, her second shot having been deflected by a Layatrebian with a shield. She halted and drew her sword and dagger intending to make a stand. She knew full well that she would probably die, outnumbered and overwhelmed by the attackers who were much bigger and stronger. The fourth and final warship landed, and her troops disembarked unopposed. The Volcanadian defenders were too busy fighting for their lives to repel them. The attackers were only three or four strides away from Joanna, when suddenly, several of the Layatrebians were struck violently to the ground. Joanna looked on with shock as more and more enemy soldiers fell dead on the beach. She looked down the coast to the south and saw to her joyous bewilderment that three Volcanadian ships were coming at full speed. Mounted two apiece on the front of each allied vessel were Eros's swivel launchers. Firing full blast, these fantastic weapons swept the beach mowing down every foe in their path. One of the launchers was aimed upward to contend with the Layatrebian archers in the crow's-nests of each enemy ship. The hapless Layatrebians were shredded to pieces by the salvo of fire from Eros's magnificent creation. Joanna ran down the beach to meet the Volcanadian landing parties and found herself standing before Eros himself.

"I thought you might be needing a little help" he said, gesturing to his heavy swivel-launchers. Joanna stuck her sabre into the sand and ran to hug the older gentlemen. The arriving members of the home guard charged across the beach towards the sounds of the raging battle leaving Joanna and Eros in a warm embrace.

After a moment, she pulled back from him so she could see his face. "Enos was killed" she said tremblingly, tears streaming from her eyes.

Eros nodded sadly, "I know, I felt in my heart that he was gone."

"I'm so sorry" she said, burying her face in his shoulder.

"Come child. We must postpone our grieving. You have done well, but the fight is not yet over."

The Volcanadian army began to fall back towards the barricades. Open ground was the last place to be during a cavalry charge. Jairus was helping a wounded comrade when he heard the horn that signaled the Alfabetian charge. The western sky was reddened to the shade of blood by the setting sun. A fitting backdrop for the army that was coming to destroy the Volcanadians. Jairus looked on with defiance at the enemy approach.

"Let them come" he thought to himself. "I may die, but I'll gladly take a few more of them with me." He was just about to turn and retreat to the fortifications when something odd caught his eye. A shadow of some sort appeared to be rising from the woods behind the Alfabetians. Like a flock of birds taking flight, but bigger, big enough to block out a large portion of the sunset.

"What the devil is that?" Marek shouted to no one in particular. As the enemy cavalry drew closer, the swarm of unknown creatures followed close behind. The black, cat-like beasts began diving at the Alfabetians, knocking them out of their saddles and sending them tumbling across the ground. This ferocious and unexpected attack brought the charging cavalry to a halt as they stopped to face their winged attackers. The sight of this brought hope to the hearts of the Volcanadians and they turned to meet the attacking infantrymen with renewed strength. Even so, the sheer numbers of Eleminos's army was more than the defenders could bear. Many good Volcanadian men had fallen, and those who remained were plagued with fatigue. Jairus and his comrades were fighting hard not to lose ground, yet they continued to be pushed back. Suddenly, a thunderous shout echoed through the valley catching the attention of every member of the conflict.

"TRRROOOOOOGG!"

Heads were turned to see the source of the battle-cry and see it they did. Lining the ridge to the south were hundreds of fierce-looking warriors. Both men and women, clad in animal skins, streaked with war-paint, and brandishing all manner of weapons from clubs to swords. The leader of the band was unmistakable. He was a man of daunting proportions wearing a cloak of bearskin and swinging a double-bladed battleax.

Chapter 20

A Hard-Earned Triumph

The Volcanadians, Alfabetians, and Layatrebians all looked at each other with apprehension. The battle stalled for a moment as everyone wondered who these newcomers would side with. The Troglodotians fixed this problem when they charged at the Alfabetians, alleviating any doubt of where their allegiances lay. The woodlanders continued to shriek all manner of battle-cries that were nearly as unnerving as their appearance. The battlefield was in utter chaos as the forces of four nations clashed together in this mighty struggle. The soldiers of Layatreb were the first to withdraw from the fight. The outcome of the battle was growing unsure, so they turned and retreated to the safety of their city's walls. The Alfabetians too were losing faith in their chances at success. They had come expecting an easy victory, but now they had begun to realize that the tide was turning.

Leif cleaved his way through the droves of Alfabetians, his hefty blade soiled from the effusion of blood. He found himself engaged with two foes at once, big brutes, one with a spear and the other a broadsword. So preoccupied was he with the adversaries before him that he failed to notice an enemy cavalryman approaching him from behind. The horseman was bearing down on Leif with a raised javelin aimed for his exposed back. Leif had just glimpsed the oncoming danger when a short-handled battleax sailed through the air and plunged deeply into the soldier's chest. The man dropped the javelin and grasped the protruding ax as he fell from his mount. Leif looked to identify his savior and saw that it had been Attimara who had thrown the ax. She was now being set upon by an oversized infantryman with only her dirk and buckler to defend herself. Leif ducked under a jab from the spear carrier and slammed the pommel of his sword into the man's forehead. Then he whirled around to deflect a slash from the Alfabetian swordsman and finished the man off with a crosscut to the throat. With his opponents dealt with, Leif heaved his sword at the man attacking Attimara. The heavy blade ran clear through the man's midsection and he dropped to the ground. Attimara withdrew the sword from the fallen soldier and threw it to Leif who in turn threw her ax back to her. They exchanged no words, but the looks on their faces spoke of gratitude and admiration. Turning back to the conflict, the two of them ran side-by-side into the thick of the battle.

Attimara's father was perhaps the fiercest warrior on the battlefield. Veteran soldiers in the Alfabetian ranks fell back when faced with the mighty chieftain. All those who unwisely made the attempt to best the Trog were quickly dispatched by a swing of his ax. Four Alfabetian cavalrymen turned their attention to Atticus intent on bringing him down. Killing the immense the Trog would bring them great honor, as well as hope to rest of their men. He turned as they charged him and let fly with the dirk from his belt. The heavy dagger struck the first rider and pierced his heart; he was dead before he hit the ground. The second soldier was knocked from the saddle by a crushing blow from Atticus's battleax. The third rider tried to run him down with his galloping horse. Atticus grabbed the charging steed's bridle and threw the beast to the ground, rider and all. The dazed horseman was then grabbed by the collar and thrown bodily through the air, knocking the fourth and final Alfabetian from his mount. "Don't mess with a Trog" Atticus said haughtily.

There are many words to describe war, and the word "quiet" is not one of them. The air was filled with what old soldiers called the song of battle. It isn't a very nice song, the subject of it being violence and suffering. The song has no words and no perceptible melody, but it does have a variety of instruments. The clashing of swords and other weapons or the grunting and snarling of warriors locked in combat. The sickening sound of metal hacking at flesh or of bones breaking under heavy blows. The pitiful cries of wounded animals and the gut-wrenching moans of men in the throes of death. In the beginning, the battle song has a sustained crescendo and then transitions swiftly to a calando until the symphony of death draws to a close over a field of bodies.

Bartimaeus soared high over the battlefield clinging to the back of a large banther. He had been forbidden from taking part in the battle because of his wound, but he maintained that he had the right to observe. He had flown in with the flock that had attacked the Alfabetian cavalry. Despite the wishes of his Trog physician, he had directed his mount to fly low over the battlefield so he could take a few shots with his short launcher. Having used all of his ammunition, Bartimaeus ascended to his current altitude where he was relatively safe from enemy archers and also had a good view of the battle. The conflict seemed to be losing some of its intensity as soldiers grew tired and retreated. He glided down towards the eastern edge of the battlefield and saw the familiar form of his mentor Eros. Bartimaeus steered his banther down to land next to his old friend and dismounted before the creature's paws touched the ground. Eros's weary face brightened at the sight of his apprentice.

"Praises to God for your safe arrival" Eros exclaimed as he and the boy embraced. Bartimaeus winced from the sting of his tender wound but hugged the man tighter regardless.

"What are you doing here?" Bartimaeus asked in wonder. "And who controls Volcanadas?"

"Drackus still leads the defense of the city." Explained Eros. "And I felt that my services could be of more use here."

Bartimaeus nodded at this, and then asked the question that plagued his mind.

"Where is the King?"

Eros looked sadly into the hopeful eyes of his young friend. He said nothing, but Bartimaeus knew the answer.

"What of Jairus and Joanna? He asked fearfully.

"Both were alive at the start of the battle… Now? I don't know" Eros said.

Chapter 21

A Soldier's Prayer

Jairus was bleeding badly from a gash on the side of his head. He picked up a handful of dry earth and pressed it into the wound to staunch the flow of blood. Marek limped over to him and sat down in the grass, sighing with exhaustion as he did.

"That scum Rotiart really knows how to throw a party" Marek joked tiredly. The battle was over at long last, the Alfabetians had finally turned to retreat. But though the encounter was finished, there was still much to do. Night was falling quickly and the dead and wounded needed tended to.

Deceased soldiers of Alfabetia and Layatreb were left to lay where they had been struck. There were more than enough allied soldiers to deal with. Let Rotiart and Eleminos collect their own dead. The fallen among the Troglodotians were borne into the sky by the banthers. The faithful creatures would carry the warriors home so they could be interred in ancestral caves, as was the tradition among their people. Dead Volcanadians were gathered and carried reverently down to the beach. Each body was identified, and the names recorded. Then the worthy departed were moved to the deck of a Volcanadian ship. This ship's hold was filled with appropriated hay and scrap wood from the barricades to serve as tinder and fuel. The ship was then towed out from the coast by another vessel and set to the torch. The dark of the night was disrupted by the fiery glow as the ship blazed. The comrades of the deceased watched as the flaming craft slipped beneath the waves, committing to the sea those brave warriors who had been lost.

Eber stood before those of his legions that remained, as well as their allies. "My people…My friends… Please join me as I speak to our creator." Eber bowed his head and began. "Our Lord God in heaven… We give thanks for the victory you bestowed on us this day… Those of us who survived are grateful for your deliverance… And we ask that you make a special place in your kingdom for those that we lost… Please forgive us dear Lord… For the abominable acts that we were inclined to commit… Let us be at peace with ourselves after the spilling of so much blood… And the loss of so many that we held dear… Please bless us as we travel home… And once again I ask… Please grant us peace."

Much of the army and all of the wounded were loaded onto the Volcanadian and Layatrebian ships for the trip home. Many would still have to travel overland, but there were enough unihorns and captured horses for everybody to ride. Most of the Trog would be returning to their woodlands, but Atticus, Attimara, and a few others would be riding along. Marek too would be joining the column headed for Volcanadas. He feared that there would be repercussions if he returned to his own city and had graciously accepted Jairus' offer to come live with the Volcanadians. Jairus himself couldn't wait to get home. The last few days had been the longest of his life and he wanted nothing more than to fall into the comfort and safety of his mother's arms.

Rotiart cowered in the corner of his chambers. The other occupant of the room was so enraged that the chubby ruler of Layatreb feared he would soon be killed. This man consumed by rage was none other than Eleminos of Alfabetia. He paced the floor like a wounded animal gone mad, and indeed, maybe he was mad.

An Alfabetian Croph

"You stupid, pathetic, imbecile" Eleminos sneered contemptuously. "Your whole idiotic plan has completely come undone. My army is weakened and the Volcanadians are retreating to protect their city. You promised me Volcanadas and you have FAILED!" His cold eyes were filled with a hatred like few had ever seen. Rotiart was trembling as he responded to the livid warlord.

"It seems that my advisors underestimated the Volcanadians, and I had no knowledge of their woodland allies. Furthermore, traitors from my own city warned Eber about the attack foiling the element of surprise."

Eleminos scoffed disgustedly. "So, what you wish for me to believe... is that none of this is your fault?

Rotiart didn't dare reply. He just stood there cringing, waiting for the penalty that befalls those who disappoint Eleminos. The Alfabetian King drew his croph, a traditional weapon of Alfabetia, and he twirled it about with a rotation of his wrist. Rotiart shivered at the sight of the razer-edge blades on the fork-like weapon.

"Perhaps my plan was flawed" he offered, sniveling as the croph was held towards his throat. "But I did manage to kill Enos. I killed the King of Volcanadas just as you requested." Eleminos nodded. "And that is the only reason I haven't already taken your head."

Chapter 22

Coronation

Jairus stood at attention in the teeming courtyard of the castle wearing the crisp new uniform of a legionnaire and his hand resting on his freshly polished rapier. It had been a week since the last of the Volcanadian troops had arrived at home. When they got there, they found that the Alfabetian siege parties had pulled up stakes and retreated into the wilderness. The following days were spent repairing damages, restocking the arsenal, and mourning the losses of the brave souls who had died in battle. But today both labor and sorrow would be set aside and replaced with celebration. The coronation of Eber, the Crown Prince of Volcanadas was indeed something worth celebrating. Jairus had been given the honor of being part of the ceremony acting as an escort for Eber when he entered the courtyard. As he waited for the service to begin, he scanned the crowds looking for his friends. Not surprisingly, Leif was standing with the guests from the Trog. He seemed to be quite taken with the girl Attimara and her with him. They made an odd-looking couple to be sure with Leif's oversized frame clad in a legionnaire's uniform standing next the five-foot woodland princess in a striking dress of jackelot skin.

"Odd-looking, yet adorable" Jairus thought with a smile. Atticus, the Trog chieftain, seemed to disagree. He stood looming behind Leif, glaring at the intertwined hands of the two smitten youths. The troubled man looked as though he wanted to break Leif's neck. Jairus was certain that the only thing preventing this was the occasional glance of reassurance from Attimara to her father. Bartimaeus was easy to find as well since he also was a part of the ceremony. Barty had his hands gripped eagerly on a swivel launcher, one of several positioned on the castle wall for the purpose of firing a salute for our new king. Thus far, Jairus had been unable to spot Joanna in the crowd, but he did have a plan of how to do so. All he had to do was keep an eye on Marek. The former soldier of Layatreb simply couldn't keep his eyes off of her, so all Jairus had to do was periodically check Marek's line of sight. Realizing he hadn't done this for several minutes, Jairus turned his head slightly to check up on the man. The Layatrebian's mouth was agape and his eyes were fixed on the courtyard entrance.

"He's spotted her" Jairus thought to himself. Turning his head just a bit more allowed him a good view of the gate, and standing there, arm-in-arm with her father was Joanna. Jairus felt his heart skip a beat at the sight of her. She too had been granted a legionnaire's uniform but had apparently made the decision to dress in a more festive nature. She wore a gown of red silk with satin sashes of pure white. Her hair was usually tied back or in braids so as not to inhibit her fighting, but now it was cascading down her back and across her shoulders. The only normal thing about her appearance was her ever-present sabre hanging at her hip. Joanna was never one to let her guard down.

The firing of the swivel launchers marked the end of the ceremony and the beginning of a new king's reign. With his responsibilities fulfilled, Jairus made his way through the crowd to get to Joanna. He had almost reached her and was about to call her name when he was cut off by Marek.

"Lovely Joanna! You take my breath away" Marek exclaimed.

Joanna blushed slightly and offered thanks for the compliment. Jairus was just about to add his own praise when Marek interrupted.

"The dancing is about to start, and I'd love it if you would do me the honor" he said to Joanna with a slight bow. Marek unhooked his mace from his belt and took Joanna's sabre, both of which he handed off to Jairus. And just like that they were gone, having disappeared into the crowd that was moving to the dance floor. Jairus was welled up with jealousy. Joanna could dance with whomever she pleased, but he would have at least liked the chance to ask her.

"I may not be your first choice, but you could dance with me" said a voice behind him. His anguish subsided as he turned to the voice with a smile.

"You'll always be my first-choice mother" he said.

Lady Magdalyn rolled her eyes. "That's a lie" she accused, "but it was nice of you to say it anyway."

After a dance with his mother and another with one of his sisters, Jairus went hunting for another chance with Joanna. The previous dance had been with her father, but she was now once again in the clutches of Marek. Jairus stood watching them, his heart sinking to his boots. Suddenly, the Trog Attimara appeared in front of him.

"Dance with me!" she ordered bluntly. Jairus' eyes opened widely as he moved to obey.

"I thought you would be dancing with Leif" Jairus stated as they began to move with music.

"Yeah, I was… But my father told him that he should sit down for a while" she responded with a grin. Jairus laughed at the idea of his big friend being intimidated by the even bigger man.

"What about you?" Attimara queried. "Why haven't you pounced on your lady friend over there?" Jairus found that he was beginning to like the brash, forthcoming nature of the little Troglodotian.

"She seems a bit busy" Jairus observed.

Attimara seemed less than impressed with his answer.

"Do you like her?" She asked. Jairus nodded timidly. "Do you wanna dance with her?"

"Yes!" Jairus admitted.

Without another word, Attimara turned and plowed through the surrounding dancers, dragging a protesting Jairus behind her. She marched right up to Marek and Joanna.

"I wanna switch partners" she said simply. And proceeded to drag Marek away by the arm. Jairus and Joanna couldn't help but laugh at the look of surprise on Marek's face. They were together at last, and Jairus couldn't think of a single thing worth saying. He held out his hand in a silent invitation and Joanna accepted with a smile.

Eleminos stood aboard a Layatrebian ship, looking upon the distant city of Volcanadas. The sounds of music and merriment carried over the water and made him want to vomit, or kill someone, or both. He had no intention of giving up on his notions of claiming this land. He had a new plan in mind to meet this end, one that didn't depend so much on fools. The idea had come to him during the battle a week earlier, even as his troops were being defeated. The more he thought about his plan the more elaborate and tremendous it became. It would take some time, but he would be coming back to take Volcanadas and he would not tolerate another failure.

Chapter 23

Brighter Days

Jairus took a deep breath of the delightful sea air and listened to the sound of the waves far below. He was standing at the rim of his lava tube surrounded by friends, including Leif, Attimara, Barty, Marek, and Joanna. The day after the coronation festivities, Attimara had asked Leif to take her swimming and Joanna had suggested to Jairus that the Trog might enjoy dropping through the tube. Jairus had reluctantly agreed to share his secret place and now the six of them were gathered around the edge.

"I don't know about this" Bartimaeus said fearfully. "I never really cared much for hei-AAHHHHHHH!!!"

Attimara had stepped nonchalantly behind the reluctant youth and shoved him off.

"He'll thank me later" she said with a smile. With that, she vaulted onto Leif's back sending the two of them plunging down the hole after Barty. This left Jairus standing with Joanna and Marek and the two remaining boards. Marek grabbed the nearest board.

"You can ride with me Joanna" he said eagerly, much to Jairus' dismay.

"No thank you" she responded. "I'm riding with Jairus." Disappointment flashed across the young man's face, but then he just smiled and stepped off on his own. Joanna turned to Jairus. "You ready?" she asked.

He leaned in and kissed her. It was quick and impulsive, completely unplanned, and more than a bit awkward. But still, he had done it and there was no going back. He stepped back nervously to measure her reaction. Her eyes were wide open in a look of astonishment. She said nothing, but she didn't seem upset. She moved around behind him and wrapped her arms around his neck for the ride down the tube.

Just before they stepped off the edge, she whispered in his ear. "I love you too."

As they slid through the lava tube and shot out into the open space, Jairus whooped and hollered with uncontainable delight.

The end...

For now...

Fun Facts about the Volcanadian Chronicles

As was mentioned in the note at the beginning of the book, this is the very first story I have ever completed and published. The process of creating the story was a lot of fun and I thought it would be cool to share some of that process with you. Different characters and elements of the story came to fruition in odd, and sometimes humorous ways. The following notes are a chronological overview of the methods behind my madness.

Jacked-up Animals

Flarefly – Interestingly enough, this creature was actually the very first element of the story to be imagined. It came before all the characters, the plot-line, and even the title of the book. The whole idea started with a rifle-like weapon that fired flaming insects.

Unihorn – One of my favorite movies is *The Chronicles of Narnia: The Lion, the Witch and the Wardrobe* (2005) and the most epic part of the film is the massive battle between the armies of Aslan and the White Witch. During this battle sequence, a rhinoceros can be seen plowing through the enemy ranks like a locomotive. I have always loved rhinos with their monstrous size and brute strength. The idea of an army mounted on rhino-like creatures is my own dream come true.

Jackelot – I asked my youngest brother Solomon for suggestions on what type of critters I should use in the story. He put forth the idea of a creature that was a mix of a cheetah and a hare. I took his suggestion, but I altered it just a bit by mixing a jackrabbit and an ocelot. I explained to my other brother Isaac what I wanted, and he drew it up even better than I had imagined. Thus, was the creation of the jackelot.

Banther – What could be cooler than flying around on a winged-panther-bat-thingy? And once again, Isaac did a magnificent job of drawing the creature.

People & Places

Jairus – The name Jairus comes from the book of Mark, chapter 5 in the bible. Jesus visits the house of Jairus and raises a girl from the dead. When I first used the name "Jairus," Microsoft-Word did not recognize it and marked it as misspelled. I right-clicked on the name to check for other spellings and among the options given were the names "Jabirus" and "Jairo." I decided then and there that my story would begin with: "I am Jairus, eldest son of Jabirus who was the son of Jairo."

Magdalyn – This is my own variation of Magdalene, as in Mary Magdalene from the book of Matthew in the bible

Enos – This name might be mistaken as a reference to the dim-witted sheriff's deputy from *The Dukes of Hazard*. However, the name Enos is yet another biblical reference. The name comes from Genesis and belongs to one of Adam and Eve's grandsons.

Enochulus – I started writing this story the week before my final in calculus with analytic geometry. Needless to say, calculus was riding heavy on my brain at the time and it seemed only right to commemorate my completion of the course. Therefore, Enochulus is a mixture of the name "Enoch" and calculus.

Volcanadas – I got the idea of building the city on a volcano after creating the flareflies. It seemed that a bug like that should live on a volcano. There is no significance behind the "Canada" in "Volcanadas."

Leif – My younger sister Kieren has always been fascinated with the Norse explorer Leif Erikson. Using the name in my book was simply a nod to her. She is also responsible for several of the weaponry illustrations in the book.

Bartimaeus – Bartimaeus is another name from the bible.

Joanna – I have always liked the name Joanna.

Eros – I just wanted another name that started with "E"

Edwalpa – Atawallpa was a ruler of Quito in the 16th century. I needed another name that started with "E" and I decided to create a variation of the South American name.

Rotiart – Pronounced: row-she-art. This name was created by spelling "traitor" backwards.

Layatreb – Pronounced: Lay-uh-treb. This is simply an anagram of the word "betrayal."

Eleminos – When teaching the ABC's to a child, it is common for L, M, N, and O to be run together and sound like elemino. I have always found this humorous and made the spontaneous decision to name my villain Eleminos.

Alfabetia – Pronounced: alfa-bay-shuh. King Eleminos is from Alfabetia. Need I say more?

Troglodotian – Pronounced: trog-la-doh-shun. I created this word from the term "troglodyte" which means cave-dweller. I thought the connection was suitable considering that the Trog live in caves. However, there has been some concern that readers might misinterpret the meaning and mistakenly associate the Troglodotians with cave-men or Neanderthals. So, let it be understood that the Trog are intelligent human-beings that simply choose to reside in caves.

Atticus - I became quite partial to this name when reading *To Kill a Mockingbird* by Harper Lee. For those who are unfamiliar with the book, Atticus is the name of the patriarch in that story.

Attimara – The name "Amara" means unfading or imperishable. I changed it to Attimara to create a more obvious connection to the character's father.

Weapons'n'Stuff

As I created each character, I put careful thought into what type weapon I wanted them to carry. I wanted there to be variety as well as individuality. For the most part, the different types of swords are identified in the story. However, there are a few destructive implements that need a bit of further explanation.

Jairus' short swords – A rapier is a fine weapon, but I liked the idea of having heavy-bladed short swords as backup. If you look at the picture, these short-swords are a combination of a Chinese butterfly-sword and a medieval sword-breaker.

Alfabetian croph – This book was an opportunity to use a weapon design that I had imagined years ago. A weapon with three prongs like a trident, but with blades like a sword. The name croph came about quite simply. The weapon is similar to a fork. Fork spelled backwards is krof. Replace the "k" with a "c" and the "f" with "ph" and that's it.

Other Weapons

The story is meant to have a medieval theme, but I included crazy things like rapid-fire weapons and flamethrowers. The best thing about writing pure fiction is you can do whatever you want with it.

Flare-launcher – It's a rifle that shoots bugs.

Swivel-launcher – The design is based on the Gatling gun.

Flame-thrower – C'mon, who doesn't love flame-throwers? These weapons are not actually used in this story because Leif and Bartimaeus lose them in the ambush in the Dark Wood. It is likely that they will come to use in book two of the series.

Geography

Volcanadas does not technically exist, but the story is intended to have taken place in the real world. The people who created the civilization are meant to have originated from many different nations. Diversifying the inhabitants of Volcanadas opens the story to a diverse cast if it should ever be made into a movie. (Wouldn't that be awesome?) This also accounts for the wide variety of weapons used by the characters.

Inserting Volcanadas into the real world also provides an explanation for the religion within the culture. Why does Christianity exist in a fictional realm? Because the founders of the civilization came from nations with a Christian influence.

Cover Art

I struggled more with designing the book's cover than with any other part of the process. I played with several different ideas and eventually settled on the one you see before you. The leather background is a picture I took of a leather-bound bible. The knife-blade that has my name on it is a real knife that I purchased at a yard-sale.

The Central image of the front cover is intended to be like a crest or coat of arms for the Volcanadians. I tried putting all kinds of things on it including rhinoceros-heads, a variety of weapons, and a volcano. I finally decided to just keep it simple. The main thing is the flarefly in the middle. I mention specifically in the book that the insects are a symbol of Volcanadas.

About the Author

Josiah Shultz is the dashingly handsome stud who wrote this book and did not write this bio (wink). When he is not writing, he is probably reading. If he is not writing or reading, he is either asleep or wishing that he was asleep. On those days when he is not sleeping he has been known to masquerade as a college student. Much of his time that should be devoted to homework is instead spent running fire and medical calls with his local volunteer fire department. He likes to spend time with his family, enjoys movies, and couldn't live without PB&J's and mac'n'cheese. He is a born-again Christian, was homeschooled K thru 12, and is the second of seven children.